One More Time

One More Time

(...just for the fun of it!)

NOTES FROM FAIRACRES

Effie Leland Wilder

with illustrations by Laurie Allen Klein

Guideposts®

CARMEL • NEW YORK 10512

www.guideposts.org

This Guideposts edition is published by special arrangement with
Peachtree Publishers, Ltd.

Text © 1999 Effie Leland Wilder
Illustrations © 1999 Laurie Allen Klein

Jacket and interior illustrations by Laurie Allen Klein
Book design by Loraine M. Balcsik
Composition by Melanie M. McMahon

Manufactured in the United States of America

Cataloging-in-Publication Data is available from the Library of Congress

To My Readers
Bless their hearts!
and
To Marian Gordin
My tireless, patient editor
and my valued friend

Acknowledgments

I do not dare, in the rickety state of my mind, to try to list the dear people who have helped me with this volume. I would leave too many names out.

So: immense gratitude to you all, the ones who sent or told me stories, and the good people at Peachtree Publishers. You've made it possible for an old, old lady to break into print, one more time.

Thank you. *Thank* you.

E. L. W.

Author's Note

Dear Reader,

In case you start wondering, along about Chapter Three, "When does the Story start?" I will save you the trouble.

At the great age of ninety, I am plot-less! There is nary a plotline in this volume.

However, there are still plenty of happenings—funny, poignant, and (alas) sad—at FairAcres Home to keep Hattie's pen flying over the pages of her diary every night. Sometimes as she writes, she chuckles over the antics of her fellow "inmates." I hope you will, too.

E. L. W.

Contents

1

Come As You Are

July 6th

Dear Diary, I haven't forgotten you. I've just been lazy lately. I will now regale you with the following true story:

A group of ladies here at The Home have a Wednesday morning Bible study hour. Last Wednesday they asked one of the members to end the meeting with a prayer.

In her soft, ladylike Southern voice she prayed, and nobody could hear a word. They kept peeping up, under their lids, to see if her lips were still moving.

Finally, when they heard a faint "Amen," one of the ladies said, "I hope God had His hearing aid in!"

Everything reminds me of something, and many long-forgotten tidbits from my childhood seem to be coming back to me these days. Ear trumpets, for instance.

Since getting hearing aids myself I've thought a lot about my grandmother, who had to give up her beloved avocation—teaching the piano—when she was about thirty-five years old, because of severe deafness.

I never saw her without that funny kind of black horn, made of tin, I think. When you wanted to tell her something, she put the metal tube in her ear and you talked into the big round opening at the other end. Through it, she seemed to hear everything we said. We never had to repeat, as people often have to do with me now, when I'm wearing my $2,800 apparatus. I doubt her trumpet cost more than three dollars.

I remember my brother would play into the trumpet with his saxophone—a jazzy number—and Grandma's eyes would light up, and her little feet would start to dance.

They weren't pretty things, ear trumpets, but they were useful, inexpensive, and easy to locate. (I'm forever misplacing my tiny gadgets.)

Oh, there was one more plus: no batteries!

July 9th

A group of people in Drayton arranged for me to give a talk at their meeting today. *Nice* people—the kind who read my books. (Brag, brag.)

I rattled on, and they gave me a standing ovation. (I'm getting spoiled; if they don't stand up while clapping, I'm put out!)

When I got home I looked in the wall mirror to see how I had appeared to the gathering—and something wasn't right. (Not that I expect that image to be *really* right, anymore, what with the ravages of time. Not only has the image in the mirror changed, but also the macular degeneration in my eyes causes dark spots on everything I see.)

Something definitely looked amiss. I took a hand mirror and got under a bright light. Oh, dear. I had on mismatched earrings! I mean, *badly* mismatched.

I could have cried. If someone had just told me. I could have taken them off.

Vanity, thy name is Woman.
Old Age, thy name is Pitiful.

Overheard:
"It used to be called lumbago, and before that it was called rheumatism. Now it's called arthritis, and I've got it everywhere except in my eyelashes."

July 13th

All my musings on age sent me looking for a poem I wrote a few years ago:

ON AGING

They say I'm going to be eighty-four.
I feel like it's a whole lot more!
Like 102, when I'm running late
And can find one shoe but not its mate;
When I find I'm wearing mismatched hose.
When I'm having trouble with crooked toes.
When people are laughing, and I'm left out
'Cause I can't hear what the fun's about.
When I'm "down in the back," and weak in the knees,
And things are making me cough and sneeze.
There are swollen joints, and gas, and gout,
And teeth falling in, and hair falling out.

Life is rough. You'd better believe it…
But I find I'm not *quite* ready to leave it!

A positive outlook does wonders (not only internally, but I'm sure it makes it easier on those around you). So I set out to find some positive thoughts about this "adventure" of aging. Here's one that appealed to me, Dear Diary. You can see why:

Alonzo of Aragon was wont to say, in commendation of age, that age appears to be best in four things: old wood, best to burn; old

wine, best to drink; old friends, best to trust;
and old authors, best to read.
                                    —Francis Bacon

(Bless Alonzo for his thoughts and Francis for quoting him; especially the last five words.)

July 15th

Big excitement! We had to be evacuated last night!!

At dusk a huge tanker-truck turned over on the highway not far from here. The tank was punctured and a liquid started pouring out, sending fumes rising into the air. The driver was unconscious. Nobody knew what the chemical was. A cloud formed, and, lo and behold! the cloud settled right over our fair acres!

Mr. Detwiler got his orders from the Chief of Police: Evacuate. The fumes might be toxic. Mr. Detwiler did a great job, including driving a bus himself, which he had never done before.

He sent aides up and down the halls knocking on doors, saying, "Come out. Come as you are, to the lobby, at once. No time to change clothes."

It was after seven o'clock, and many of us had undressed and were relaxed, watching *Wheel of Fortune,* so it was an odd group of bath-robed oldsters who gathered in the lobby. Cornelia's thin hair looked rather pitiful. She hadn't had time to put on her wig. Emily's hair was in curlers!

I believe the local hospital helped in getting the patients out of the Health Care Center.

Mr. D had rounded up everyone except Gusta Barton. She was in bed, and refused to get out.

"I refuse to leave my comfortable bed for any old oil spill." (That's what she insisted on calling it.)

Mr. Detwiler pled with her. "Everybody else is going, Mrs. Barton. Why can't you?"

"Because I'm smarter than they are. Go on and leave me alone."

And he did. He couldn't pick her up by himself, and he didn't have time to form a posse to do it.

With those of us still "on legs" helping those on canes and walkers, we piled into the buses, and were taken to the Main Street Elementary School. Someone had alerted the nice principal, Mr. Myers, and he welcomed us into the school's cafeteria.

The chairs, made for grade-schoolers, were too small for many of us. Our posteriors overflowed.

Mr. Myers sent out for hot dogs and did all he could think of for our comfort—but it was a long night.

Cora finally announced, "I've had enough of this chair"— whereupon she climbed on one of the cafeteria's tables and stretched out. To my amazement she soon fell asleep with her hands clasped peacefully on her stomach.

Emily and Cornelia had an idea. They searched nearby classrooms. Sure enough, on one teacher's desk they found a vase of silk flowers. They purloined a few tiny flowers, made a nosegay of them, and placed it in Cora's clasped hands. I wish someone had had a camera! Soon she was snoring gently. Once in a while the snore would be a snort, and whenever this happened the bouquet in her hands would quiver. She furnished the best entertainment of that long night.

We told jokes, and sang, and did exercises. Some of the men sat at a table and wished for a deck of cards. At long, long last, when dawn was making a timid beginning, the police told Mr. Detwiler that we could go home. The cloud had floated away and dissipated.

We dragged home to a good hot breakfast and a long morning nap. The only person at FairAcres who didn't sleep this morning was Gusta. She was disgustingly bright-eyed, and seemed quite pleased with herself.

*Emily and Cornelia made a nosegay and placed
it in Cora's clasped hands.*

2

Special Deliveries

July 17th

Today was my son Ray's birthday, and that got me to remembering. The youngest of our four children—our Extra Dividend, we called him (among a few other names)—was born when I was forty-three. And wouldn't you know? He was the fastest and brashest of the lot. The neighbors had fun watching me chase him down the street. Sometimes they would come out and help "the Poor Old Soul" (my husband Sam's nickname for me, and which I felt like at the time) run him down.

It didn't do my ego any good either when people would come up to me in a store and say, "What a cute little grandson you have!"

None of it seemed to bother Sam. He just went around with his chest stuck out. Big Papa. He didn't have to chase a ball of fire from sunup to sundown. By the time Big Papa came home from work, his youngest's energy was at last on the wane. Sam couldn't understand why I looked and felt like "The Wreck of the Hesperus." Why, indeed. I will give one example.

One morning when Raymond was about three, and playing with his blocks on the floor, I left him long enough to answer the phone in the next room. The conversation only lasted about three minutes, but that was long enough for Ray to take his chance and fly the coop. I ran all over the house calling him, searching every closet. Getting panicky, I ran out on the back porch, calling his name. After a minute I spied him on top of the garage! With the help of a barrel and a tree limb he had reached the garage's roof, and was sitting on its front ledge, calmly, with his legs hanging over.

In a shaky voice I called out, "Raymond! Come down from there!"

He looked straight at me and said, "You make me nerbous." I wonder where he'd heard *that?*

Two doors down from us lived a nice sixteen-year-old boy named Robbie Dent, who was becoming famous as a high school quarterback. He heard the commotion and helped me with the rescue. Robbie had apparently paid Ray some attention, and the little tyke looked up to the teenager.

None of us realized the extent of Ray's attachment to, and regard for, this older boy until one Sunday morning when Ray was missing from his bed at seven o'clock. While we searched frantically for the little fellow—still just three years old—Robbie Dent was waking up and finding an unexpected visitor in his bed: Raymond McNair, in his pajamas, was snuggled under the covers in Robbie's bed and grinning up at him. Robbie told us later, "He scared the heck out of me, but I couldn't fuss at him to save my life!" I know just how he felt.

I finally had a chance to settle down to calmer middle age when Raymond entered school. He had looked forward to the first grade, but for some reason it didn't live up to his expectations. (Maybe because his teacher was younger and stricter than the Poor Old Soul.) Anyway, I remember one cold morning in November when Sam got up early and lit a fire in the den's fireplace. Ray stood with his back to the flames, getting a thorough warming.

After a while he announced, very calmly, "I don't think I'll go to school today. I think I'll just stay home and warm my butt." Oh, my!

It is hard to believe my rambunctious Raymond is just about the age *I* was when he was born! I sent him a card, but I must remember to call tonight and wish him a happy birthday.

Later

After lunch today, when the men had left our table (probably having heard enough "she-she" talk), we women began to compare notes about the births of our children. All of us had "delivered" in the good old days when the mandatory stay in the hospital was ten days. Ten blissful, restful days! I believe some women had the second child just to get that heavenly rest. Nowadays they throw mother and child out almost as soon as they get the cord cut.

Marcia's story was different.

"I didn't go to a hospital when my child was born," she said. We looked at her in amazement.

"You see, my sister was a nurse, and she married a doctor, and they lived on the outskirts of a small town upstate. The Depression was still on. Times were hard, and I was delighted when they asked me to come to their house for the birth. I was glad to get a Rural Free Delivery!"

July 20th

Curtis and Paul were ruminating and smoking on the terrace tonight, and I was listening at the library window.

They were talking about the plans for the swimming pool that is being built as a result of the money Paul won in a national car-naming contest last spring.

"How d'you think it's looking?" asked Curtis.

"OK, I guess—but I'll be glad when they actually start digging.... I want to make sure I'll get to dive in, at least once."

Curtis chuckled. "I reckon I'd do a belly-buster, if I tried.... I tell you what's gonna be funny, Paul: lookin' at some of these characters here in bathin' suits. In fact, I wrote a verse last night to Madame Geneva Tinken. Wanna hear it?"

"You know I do."

"OK.

> My dear Mistress Tinken
> You've got me a-thinkin'.
> You're too string-beany
> To wear a bikini!"

Paul whooped, and so, *almost*, did I. I began to think of some other figures, including mine. I tried to picture Steven Comstock in the pool. He has expressed an interest in using it. I don't believe there is a measuring tape big enough to go around his waist. As my Sam would say, "He was built when meat was cheap." I guess he'll have to go to Omar the Tent Maker to have a pair of trunks made.

I hope the lights in that pool house will have low wattage.

July 22nd

Bill Nixon told us a funny tale today, not quite as outrageous as some of his stories.

He said four fellows were playing golf, and they were thwarted by the slowness of the men playing just ahead of them, who seemed to take forever to make every play and to find their balls.

After urging them on several times, the foursome finally went back to the clubhouse and complained.

"Oh, gentlemen," said the pro, "you mustn't fuss at those fellows! They're blind!"

Three of the four felt chagrined about having been impatient with the blind players and wanted to make amends.

Al said, "I tell you what I'll do. I'll pay their greens fees."

Henry said, "I'll pay for their cart rentals."

Joe said, "I'll buy each of 'em a drink.... How about you, Fred? Are you gonna do something for those poor blind guys?"

"Not me," said Fred. "I'm not gonna give 'em a thing. They could-a played last night!"

Later, ruminating

Most of the people here at FairAcres are good company—like Bill, who has a knack for making us smile. But not all are as sharp as he is.

There are a few who need to make use, before launching into a soliloquy, of that invaluable inquiry:

"Have I told you this before?"

We might call that inquiry the Six Bless-ed Words. Better still: the Lifesaving Question. It allows the listener to nod his head politely and ward off having his head nod involuntarily later, in sleepy boredom.

July 25th

Emily just got back from visiting her sister Ella in Mississippi. While she was there they learned that a very elderly aunt named Maria was talking about moving in with Ella. She groaned at the thought of the responsibility, but her young son said, generously and blithely, "Oh, don't worry so much, Mama. Aunt Maria is low maintenance."

I think I might like that young man.

～

We accused Emily of bringing back some especially hot "Mississippi-style" summer weather. It has been sweltering, and we are all grateful for the modern invention of air-conditioning!

Julia made us laugh today, remembering aloud something her mother had told her.

Julia's mother, Helen, came from a very small Southern town where a big occasion, every summer, was "Protracted Meeting," a week of religious services held in a tent, in the hottest week in July.

Helen said her sister Ruth was trying to iron something to wear to the Protracted Meeting, and perspiration was dripping from her forehead onto the ironing board. Finally she pulled the dress off the board in frustration.

"I'll tell you something," she said. "It's just *too hot* to *protract!*"

The new swimming pool, we all agreed, will be most welcome this time of year. I must ask Paul when it is scheduled to be finished.

3

A Distressing Development

July 27th

My friend Louisa ("Louly") Canfield had a rather severe stroke over the weekend and is in the Health Care Center. Louly has been at this Home nearly as long as I have, and we've become good friends. I'm distressed about her, especially since she has no close family left, to "do" for her. She was never married.

I've always been so proud of Louly for what she did to help Arthur Priest, our beloved maintenance man. Hearing that he could not get a driver's license because he had dyslexia and couldn't read, she set herself up as his teacher, taught him to read, and enhanced his life thereby. (A story that I wrote about a few years ago.)

With his new license, he was able to drive The Home's vehicles, and the administration soon made him head of the Maintenance Department.

July 29th

Sometimes I scold myself for being slow or clumsy or awkward. Sometimes I even vow to try to make improvements. For instance, if my left hand drops something or fails to cut something or open something properly, I say to myself, "I must work with my left hand. I *must* start training it to function properly." And then I have a sad thought: Isn't it a little late to start such a course of improvement?! What semester in the school of life do you think you're in, old girl?

I keep forgetting.

Later

When I went to check on Louly today, Arthur and Dolly were just leaving. I could see the loving concern in their faces for their kindly and patient benefactor. They said that they would bring the children to visit as soon as Louly felt stronger.

August 1st

I usually fix a light breakfast in my kitchenette, but this morning I woke up earlier than usual, and felt I had the energy to dress and go to the dining room. I'm glad I did.

Three of us got to talking about women's church meetings a long time ago. This was when the Women of the Church were called the Auxiliary. In my mother's time I believe they were the Ladies' Aid.

Anyway, they were later divided into groups called circles, and it was about a circle meeting that Cora regaled us this morning.

She said she sat by the oldest member, Minnie Holder, who looked a little disheveled.

"How're you doing, Minnie?" Cora asked.

"Not so good. Something happened this morning that upset me."

"What was that?"

"I had a phone call from Bessie. 'How're you, Min?' she asked. 'Not good,' I answered. 'Whatsa matter?' she said. 'I can't find my telephone,' I said. 'Oh,' Bessie said, 'then I'd better hang up and let you look for it....' Something about that conversation has worried me all day."

"Poor old Min," recounted Cora. "She looked so distressed that we really tried not to laugh, but I saw a number of bowed heads and shaking shoulders. She had *made* the circle meeting."

August 2nd

Intriguing song heard on the radio: "A Soft Place to Fall." I just heard the end of it, those five words. Now I'm curious about the rest of it.

Unfinished snatches of songs, of poems, of college cheers pop into my flaky mind at the oddest times. This, for instance:

> You can bring Rose
> With the turned-up nose,
> But *don't* bring Lulu!

What is it? Where did it come from? It's been driving me crazy all morning. Poor Lulu! Why couldn't she be brought?

~

Good advice: If you can't go to your class reunion as a thin person, for goodness sake, try to go as a rich one.

Our simmering weather continues, prompting the following:

> WHEW!

> Ladies, they say, don't perspire,
>   They merely gently glow.
> I thought I was a lady
>   But now—well, I don't know.

> In this outrageous heat wave
>   I hope it doesn't show
> That in plebeian fashion
>   I'm drowning in the "glow"!

A memory:

It was hot midsummer, and Sullivan's Island with its lovely beach, across the harbor from Charleston, was filled with vacationers. All owners or renters of beach houses found suddenly that they possessed a myriad of friends who couldn't wait until fall to see them, but had to make the trek to the "oilun," as they pronounced it. Such visitors were easily persuaded to "stay over" and sleep in the breeze, on bed, cot, sofa, or hammock. (This was the era well before air-conditioning.)

Sam and I were renters ourselves, and well acquainted with the problem of drop-in company who stayed on for supper. I had often had to stretch a small can of salmon into a large salad with anything that I could find in the back of the "ice box."

Therefore, we thoroughly enjoyed witnessing this scene one Saturday while buying provisions at Simmons's Grocery.

A uniformed maid came in to use the public telephone—very public, just hanging on the wall where everyone in the little store could overhear. She dialed a number and in a loud voice passed along instructions from her employer to the prospective guests:

"Miss Mary say, if y'all comin' to the beach t'day, she say y'all please bring some delicatess."

Ever afterward, the ingredients of a Sunday night supper—salami, rye bread, cheese, and so (drool) on— had a fine name at our house. Delicatess. Isn't it perfect?

August 3rd

I hate to complain, but this morning a bunch of do-gooders came out to see us. One of them came up to me. "How *are* you, dear?" she asked, grinning, and grabbed my arthritic hand in a grip that nearly made me scream. That hand ached for hours.

I thought: The first thing that do-gooders should learn is how to shake an old person's hand.

~

A questionable compliment: "That's a pretty dress you're wearing. I've *always* liked it."

August 4th

I saw Curtis and Paul walking from the dining room toward the terrace for their smoke-and-chat session, so I headed for that window in the library where I could listen.

They talked quietly about the weather for a while, and then Curtis started to chuckle.

"Tell me what's funny," said Paul.

"Well—I was just rememberin' something that happened when I was a kid, back when people had servants.

I headed for that window in the library where I could eavesdrop on Curtis and Paul.

My father was a large, impressive man, with a commanding voice. Everybody respected him.

"He had to go to Washington on business, and on the morning of the day he was to return I overheard the cook talking to the yard man.

"'You know somethin', man? The Boss is comin' home today. Whoo-eee! Us got to p on our q's!!'"

I thought Paul would die laughing. My shoulders shook, too.

Then Paul told Curtis one.

"You know something, Curtis," Paul said, lowering his voice until I almost couldn't hear the joke. "There's a regular epidemic of AIDS at this place."

"*What?*"

"It's true. And some people have them in *both* ears!"

Later

Oooooo, Dear Diary, I have a story I'd surely like to tell to Paul and Curtis. It's just their style (although, of course, I don't dare reveal my chronic eavesdropping on their story-swapping sessions.)

My informant vows and declares this happened in Georgia.

Members of the congregation of a small-town Methodist church took turns inviting the elderly preacher to Sunday dinner.

One Sunday the hostess and her husband excused themselves to finish the dinner preparations and left the minister in the parlor with their small son, Wilbur.

"I'll bet you can't guess what we're havin' for dinner," said Wilbur.

"Well, let's see," said the preacher. "Is it fried chicken?"

"Nope."

"Is it smothered chicken?"

"Nope."

"Is it baked chicken?"

"Nope."

"Is it...*could* it be..." he looked hopeful... "roast beef?"

"Nope. I'll tell you. It's buzzard. I heard Mama say 'I guess it's time we had the old buzzard for dinner.'"

I think I'll go and visit Louly tomorrow. She'll enjoy these stories.

4

Pros and Cons

August 7th

Last year the ladies of the Drayton Garden Club started a nice project for FairAcres Home: in an empty space around the fountain behind Main Hall they put in a garden that would attract butterflies.

They planted milkweed, asters, verbena, buddleia, and cornflowers, and the butterflies came: swallowtails, fritillaries, cabbage whites, and monarchs. The butterflies seem to love the spot, and we love to sit among them, or watch them through the huge picture window in the lobby.

Yesterday Mother Nature treated us to one of those benevolent August days, a welcome break in the heat, and some of us decided to spend an hour of the summer daylight after supper in the Butterfly Garden. Our nice Mr. Detwiler—the best of administrators—saw to it that comfortable benches were placed in the center, near the fountain. There we sat, watching the lovely "critters" do their fluttering act.

Talk turned to the old-fashioned flowers that we remembered, growing up. Often the names they went by were so picturesque.

"I remember 'butter-and-eggs' and 'lords and ladies,'" Retta said.

"Oh, and there was something called 'Quaker ladies,'" Emily added.

"A shrub called 'Devil's walking stick' made an impression on me," laughed Graham McKnight. "I only had to touch that thorny stem once, and I never forgot that name! But my favorite plant was one my mother had—something called 'Dutchman's-breeches.' The flowers looked like tiny pantaloons."

"This place reminds me of my grandmother's garden," said Cora. "It was quiet like this, and she grew some of the same flowers. She had what she called a 'pit,' covered with glass—a cold frame, I guess—where she put some of her plants in the winter. Even in the coldest months she always had fresh flowers for the house: japonicas, mostly (now called camellias). There were trellises and an old well that she had covered with Confederate jessamine vines. It was so peaceful.... I loved visiting at her house."

"Peaceful and *cold*, I'll bet, in winter," spoke up Graham. "I remember visiting my grandparents, and shivering while I put on my union suit in front of a 'trash burner.' No furnace. Man, was it cold! And then, when we'd come in the summer, we'd burn up. They had one big electric fan, and we'd move it from one room to another.... Don't talk to me, Cora. You can *have* the old days."

Well, that started such a discussion that I wished for a tape recorder. Here are a few remarks I remember:

"I'm with you, Graham. My grandmother had to wash clothes in a wringer-washer."

"Mine didn't. She hired someone for that kind of work," Emily said.

"So," countered Graham, "the outside help had the back-breaking job. Now everyone can drop the clothes in a machine and press a button. Tell me that's not better!"

"I know what you mean," said Esther. "When I think about what I went through to get a permanent wave! They rolled my poor locks and hooked them up to this prehistoric electrical machine that raised my eyebrows—literally—and you could smell the hair burning. When my scalp would start smoking they'd fan me!

I'd be a kinky-headed wreck when it was over. Now they do it in half the time, with chemicals—*cool* chemicals, for half the price."

Retta and I joined in the laughter as we recalled our own experiences with that machine.

"I know," admitted Cora. "Lots of things are better. But some big things are worse, like crime, and traffic, and noise...and manners...."

"Well," said Bill Nixon, "there's a lot to be said for the slower, kinder, quieter good old days. But I can name you two things—just two things—that stop the argument in its tracks: penicillin and air-conditioning."

Graham nodded. "But, Bill, you'll *have* to add the telephone and television...."

Most of us had to nod our heads at that. We *are* living better and longer and more comfortably.

Still...I'm glad I was born early enough in this century to remember a more leisurely and (let's face it) a *sweeter* way of getting through the days.

August 8th

After our conversation about the "good ol' days" and "good new days," I hunted up some doggerel verse I remembered writing—back in the mid-eighties, I think—about a couple of "modern mistakes" (in my humble opinion):

LAMENT

It's not a rumor. It's not a joke.
They've gone and Pepsi'd-up my Coke!
I feel distressed and violated.
Someone should be annihilated
For messing around with The Real Thing.
What they're teaching the world to sing
Is: Make it sweeter, make it cloying,
Leave an aftertaste annoying.
Cut down on that lovely fizziness.
Anything to "up" the business.
"It needed fixing" is the word they've spoken.
Here's what gets me: It wasn't broken!

TWO GEMS

Two gems we had, so it seemed to me:
Coca-Cola and AT&T.
So what do we dummies do? Oh, brother!
We mess up one and break up the other!

Thank goodness, so many people lamented about the change in Coca-Cola that the company had to get that old formula out of the safe again.

The situation with telephone service, however, has continued to get more and more confusing. I now get *two* bills instead of one, and each bill is several pages long. There's always some mysterious, new fee, and, it seems to this Old Soul, the totals are always going *up*, never down! Oh, me.

August 11th

Still to my astonishment, I'm getting "fan mail" in response to my little books—618 letters, as of yesterday. Some of the letters are from men, and some of the men have sent me stories that I can't clean up enough to use. I don't want my mother rolling over in her grave any more than she has already done since I started scribbling in my diary and getting my jottings published.

I had an amazing letter the other day from a lady in a far-off state (Ohio? Kansas?). She said she lives in a retirement community, but her mother does not! Her mother, aged ninety-six, stays on the "old place," and refuses to go to any kind of a "home." My correspondent said, "Instead of my going to see her in a retirement home, she comes to see me! She says she wants to die under her own roof."

I admire the older lady's determination. I just hope her roof holds out, and her back steps, and her legs.

Later

Ruth had a good, true story to tell today, about the sale of her house when she was getting ready to come here.

She said the For Sale sign had only been up a few hours when Dr. Stevens (her physician) called her real estate agent and offered to buy the house. He told the Realtor that he was ready to deal if Ruth would come down fifteen thousand dollars on the price.

Ruth said to her agent: "You tell Dr. Stevens that when I went to his office last month, he charged me forty dollars for the office visit, and fifteen dollars for the vitamin shot. I paid his bill without a single word of argument."

Dr. Stevens got the message. The next day they drew up a contract on the house—at her asking price.

August 13th

Observed:

I passed Harriet in the hall, just as she was balling up her hometown paper to throw away.

"Nothing in here for me," she said. "I don't even read the obituaries anymore. They're all younger than I am."

She walked to the wastebasket and threw the paper in, resentfully.

August 15th

We have a few oddballs here. I suppose it is to be expected, with a population ranging from 70 to 99 years of age, with one woman of 102.

I'm continually surprised by what some of them say and do. Today I went to walk in the Butterfly Garden again and found Esther Pickett sitting on one of the benches, looking sad, with tears running down her cheeks.

"What's the matter, Esther?" I asked, sitting down beside her and rummaging in my handbag for a clean tissue.

She sniffled into the tissue and brushed her cheeks with her fingers. "Just something silly," she said, looking away from me. "You wouldn't believe how silly."

"Try me."

"Well, to tell you the truth, Hattie, I was feeling sad about chickens."

"*Chickens?*"

"Yes. I just read a newspaper article about the ones that are being born today in those chicken factories. The chickens whose feet never touch the ground."

We were quiet for a minute, and I searched for a response. "I suppose it *is* sad," I admitted. "They are raised on wire, aren't they?"

"'Deed they are. I was in one of those factories a few years back. About a million poor creatures squawking away, with about ten inches of space apiece, and their feet on a wire floor. It killed me to think that their feet would never feel the ground, not *once.*"

"But Esther," I patted her hand, "they don't know what they're missing if they've never experienced it—"

"I know. But I'm still sad. You see I used to visit my grandmother, and she always had such *happy* chickens—"

"How do you know they were happy?"

"You could *tell:* they were fat and sassy, and each one of them strutted around like she owned that chicken yard. The darling little 'biddies' had fun, scratching away. They had a stout house at the back of the chicken yard to go into at night or when it rained or was cold. That's where the hens' nests were. They knew that Grandma, or I, would be there on time, flinging out good food to them...."

"So they would get fat and be good for you to eat," I said, pointedly.

"But they didn't know that was coming! They ran around on the warm ground, pecking and cackling.... I used to hate it when the cook would catch one and wring her neck—but at least the little bird had enjoyed her short life, on earth...I mean *really* on earth, on the ground, not on *wire!*"

The last word was a wail. I patted her hand again and made a few more consoling comments as I rose and moved on.

With all the things we old people have to be sad about, it had never occurred to me to grieve about the life of modern-day chickens. Oh, well...to each his own. I walked away, shaking my head and musing about the oddities of human nature. I decided a cup of coffee was in order. Maybe I could find a less distraught companion in the Country Store.

Sure enough, when I got to that emporium just off of our lobby, I saw Paul Chapin at one of the tiny tables, having coffee and a doughnut.

"I skipped lunch," he said, "and found I couldn't wait until supper." He held up his fried doughnut. "Sit down and be sinful with me, Hattie."

So I did. There's something very comforting about Paul. Soon I was telling him about Esther shedding tears over the chickens' plight. He didn't laugh.

"Poor Esther," he said, and stirred his coffee reflectively. "Hers must be a soft heart. That organ can be touched in the most surprising ways...."

He looked as if he were remembering something from long ago. I hoped he would tell it, but after a moment he changed the subject. I did not press him. We share some of our memories here, but not all.

We talked, among other things, about the swimming pool. He has promised to escort me on a walk one morning over to the site to check on the progress.

I will be the envy of some here if they see me on the arm of this distinguished, and "eligible," widower. (To *some* ladies here, *any* widower is "eligible.") I believe I can say with confidence, however, that Paul and I are quite comfortable with our "uncomplicated" friendship. He is a truly kind man, and we enjoy one another's company.

5

Senior Moments

August 20th

Some very nice person sent me this piece, and I promptly lost the name of the sender. I'm grateful to the person for some lines that are, alas, only too true.

I'M A SENIOR CITIZEN

I'm the life of the party...even when it lasts until 8 P.M.

I'm very good at opening childproof caps...with a hammer.

I'm usually interested in going home before I get to where I'm going.

I'm good on a trip for at least an hour without my aspirin, Beano, antacid.

I'm the first one to find the bathroom wherever I go.

I'm awake many hours before my body allows me to get up.

I'm smiling all the time because I can't hear a word you are saying.

I'm good at telling stories...over and over and over.

I'm aware that other people's grandchildren are not as bright as mine.

I'm so cared for: long-term care, eye care, private care, dental care.

I'm not grouchy. I just don't like traffic, waiting, crowds, children, politicians.

I'm positive I did housework correctly before my mate retired.

I'm sure everything I can't find is in a secure place.

I'm wrinkled, saggy, and lumpy...and that's just my left leg.

I'm having trouble remembering simple words like...

I'm realizing that aging is not for sissies.

I'm anti-everything now: anti-fat, anti-smoke, anti-noise, anti-inflammatory.

I'm walking more (to the bathroom) and enjoying it less.

I'm going to reveal what goes on behind closed doors...absolutely nothing!!

I'm sure they are making adults much younger these days.

I'm in the initial stage of my Golden Years: SS, CDs, IRAs, AARP...

I'm wondering...if you're only as old as you feel, how could I be alive at 150?

I'm a walking storeroom of facts...I've just lost the storeroom.

Do I have Alzheimer's? I don't remember. But, I'm happy, I think.

I'm a senior citizen, and I think I am having the time of my life!!

August 21st

As I was coming back from seeing Louly in the Health Center, I was nearly toppled by a resident who was walking down the hall and weaving from one wall to the other. She wasn't intoxicated; the poor soul is just unsteady. She's what we call a "weaver."

One of the maintenance men, who happened by at the same time, came to my rescue and helped me keep my balance. The cause of the collision continued obliviously on her way.

"That lady is tackin' in the wind—and there ain't no wind!" my rescuer said to me, chuckling.

~

Overheard later:

First man: "I'll tell you something, friend: graveyards are just gettin' too full! Soon they'll have to start buryin' people on the perpendicular—standin' up—to save room."

Second man: "What they'll have to do, then, is put out a sign: 'SRO—Standing Room Only.'"

August 24th

New residents—Donald and Mary Dinwiddy—are easy to know, and they are making friends here rapidly.

I asked them today if they had children. Donald said, "We have one daughter, Alice, who lives in California, alas. We see her and her family about once a year, if we're lucky. And then, in Raleigh—closer to home— lives our Number One Son, David. He's our only son, but we call him Number One to keep him on his toes. After all, we could still adopt another one!"

I think I'm going to enjoy the Dinwiddys. (Or would you spell it 'Widdies'?)

August 30th

I've been "down in the back" for a few days, and was beginning to feel sorry for myself when Retta came to

see me. She is such good company that my back began
to feel better right away. I'll always be glad she chose
FairAcres when she gave up her house. And I know she's
glad, too. She never expected to remarry, but she and
Sidney Metcalf are a wonderful match.

"What's been happening?" I asked. "Any juicy news?"

"Not a scrap that I can think of.... Oh, there was one
kind of funny thing. I was in the front office talking to
Nan when Mr. Slocum came in—*you* know—the new
man who's not hitting on all cylinders. He said he
couldn't find his spare pair of dentures, and he thought
somebody had stolen them. 'Maybe their conscience
will start botherin' them,' he said to Nan, 'and they
might decide to turn 'em in to you; so I just thought I'd
tell you....' And he walked out. Nan and I had to giggle
a little," Retta confessed.

I had to giggle too. The things that happen at this place!

"I don't know any gossip," said Retta. "I've been staying home trying to clean out my bureau drawers and
closet, and straighten out my desk. Sidney and I are
going on a cruise this fall, and I don't want to die
embarrassed."

"I know what you mean," I said. "I've *got* to work on
mine, too.... There's a new lady on this hall from
Massachusetts, and she's always cleaning up—as if she
enjoys it! Cleaning up is a chore for me. I put it off as
long as I can."

"I do, too," agreed Retta. "But I had an aunt who was kind of Yankee-fied in that respect. Aunt Rosa was never happier than when she had a dust cloth in her hand.... Oh, Hattie, I'll have to tell you a story about her. You'll love it."

I knew I would.

"This happened a long time ago, when telephones stood upright. You remember, Hattie, the receiver you listened through hooked to the side, and you spoke into a separate mouthpiece.

"Well, Aunt Rosa's phone rang one day. She answered, and a man's voice told her that he worked for the telephone company and that they had decided to clean out the telephone lines by blowing through them. He asked if she would tie a paper bag around the phone's mouthpiece, to catch the dust. Aunt Rosa, being a believing soul and a tidy housekeeper, said she thought it an excellent idea. She hastened to comply with his suggestion, feeling very virtuous. Her feeling changed to chagrin later when, having decided the lines must now be clean, she removed the bag and replaced the receiver. The phone rang immediately and the sassy voice of her nephew sang out: 'April Fool!'"

September 8th

I have another entry about a do-gooder. I seem to be down on them, and I shouldn't be. Many of them are extremely kind and helpful. I just have run into several lately who seem to think that because of the marvelous college course they're taking (Psychology 101 or Geriatrics 102 or something) they know more about what's wrong with us, and what we need and want, than we do.

One of them talked down to me today, giving me some unsolicited and uninformed advice. I wanted to tell her that there's a very simple old saying worth remembering: Old people know more about being young than young people know about being old. I wanted to say it, Dear Diary, but I didn't.

September 10th

When it's time for our annual physical exam, most of us get a hairdo at the beauty shop; then we bathe and put on makeup and a little body powder, and maybe even a drop of perfume. After all, the doctor—often, anyway—is a *man*. (Oh, and we put on our best under-wear, which the nurse promptly has us take off, giving us a rattly paper gown to put over our nakedness.)

Thinking the matter over, I decided we were going at it all wrong. We should make ourselves look as worn-out and dragged-down as we possibly can, with leaden eyes and droopy mouth ("drap-lipped," as our old cook used to call it). We'll get more attention that way. Might even get a tonic, or a few B-12 shots, to perk us up.

September 11th

Mark Russell, speaking on TV about the Y2K matter, said: "I'm convinced it's going to happen. The year after this one will not be 2000, but will be 1900, all over again. Why? Because God is saying, 'You're going to keep on getting that miserable century until you get it right.'" Maybe Mark didn't say "miserable," but that was the idea. And when you think of two World Wars, the Holocaust, Korea, Vietnam, Jonestown, Oklahoma City, and ever-more-disgraceful political scandals, maybe he has something.

I wrote a poem about that last subject:

COLOR IT BLUSH PINK

> I always held that house in awe:
> The White House—trim, serene.
> On Pennsylvania Avenue
> It sat there like a queen.
> Well now, in Nineteen Ninety-Eight
> It's lost some of its glow.
> It's not the shining residence
> That children learn to know.
> To me, it's slightly tarnished.
> And isn't that a shame?
> I'd like to call the Occupant
> An un-Presidential name!
> (Oh, to have Harry Truman back!)

That reminded me of another commentary I wrote on the politics of our country:

SUMMER '88

Election year! It's fairly sickening,
All of the endless politick-ening.
Turn on the TV and pay the tolls.
Promises, promises, platforms and polls.
England is smarter. It gives to each peer
Only three weeks to electioneer.
Too many Mamas have said to a son:
"You could grow up to be President, Hon."
So Hon grows up and gets ambitious
(And sometimes a little too big for his britches).
Oh, me! The carryings-on and contentions!
And we haven't even reached the conventions!

September 12th

Paul and I finally took our walk to the swimming pool this afternoon after lunch. The project should be completed in a few weeks. There was so much "to-do" when Paul won first prize in the contest and vowed to use the money for a pool that he has decreed *no* celebration for the opening.

6

Friends

September 13th

A few months ago a couple named Edgar and Martha Cruickshank moved into one of The Home's cottages. They entered younger than most people; he is seventy-three, she was sixty-eight. They came early because of her ailing heart. One morning, soon after their arrival, he woke up and found that she had died in the night.

He was devastated. They had no children, and they were everything to each other. I don't think I've ever seen a more devoted couple, which is sweet and lovely until the inevitable *denouement* occurs.

Nobody could console "Mr. C," as he had come to be called. (Cruickshank was too long, and no one felt quite close enough to call him Edgar or Ed.) Any number of us tried without success to get him to play cards, or go to a movie, or go to the chapel services. Once in a while he would come to a meal, looking disheveled, and he rarely spoke to anyone. The chaplain tried to get him interested in delivering Meals-on-Wheels, and in other charitable projects, to no avail.

Mr. C lost weight, and began to look untidy. It really began to appear as if the man would die of grief. We don't need that kind of sadness in *this* place.

And then something fortuitous occurred, just in time! One day Mr. C phoned the maintenance department and said that his refrigerator was not working properly.

Arthur Priest, our esteemed maintenance man, went over immediately. With him on this day (it was summertime) was one of his boys, Clifton (often called "Cliffie"), aged six.

Cliffie is a winning kind of child: quiet, but with a ready smile—a very special, sweet, appealing expression that lights up his eyes. Everybody here loves to make Cliffie smile.

While Arthur worked on the refrigerator, the old man and the little boy "became acquainted." Cliffie sat quietly, and Mr. C apparently felt a call, a pleasant call, to entertain him. I wasn't there, but I can picture Mr. C searching for something to amuse his nice young visitor, sitting so quietly. He must have found something good, because Cliffie came back the next day by himself. ("Kudzu Kottage," where he lives, is just off of our campus, and is an easy and safe walk to The Home's cottages.)

We began to see the old man and the little boy walking around the grounds, feeding the ducks, skipping rocks on the water, and fishing in the duck pond. We heard that Mr. C got permission to take Cliffie to the Edisto River, where the fishing is much more exciting.

Soon the boy was a regular visitor. From time to time we would spot him playing with toys his new friend had made for him: a slingshot, and a bow and arrow. The two of them would sit for hours at a table in the cottage yard, laughing and playing slapjack or Go Fish. They even got down on the ground and played mumblety-peg.

Mr. C started coming to more meals. He dressed more carefully, and he shaved more often. On Saturdays he would often bring Cliffie with him to lunch in our dining room. Everybody went out of their way to greet them and encourage the friendship.

Sometimes we would see them giggling together over some joke. Mr. C—cleaned up—is an unusually nice-looking man, and Cliffie, with his laughing eyes and the cowlick in the front of his hair, is an adorable child.

We're pushovers here for visiting children anyway; and this one—Arthur's son Clifton—was special.

Today on my afternoon walk I passed close to the Cruickshank cottage and saw Mr. C and his small pal in the yard. They spied me, and Mr. C called me over. He and Cliffie were terribly excited about something. Cliffie was jumping up and down.

"Come see what we found, Miss Hattie!" said the old gentleman with more life in his voice than I had ever heard before. "Cliffie here has dug up a treasure!"

"They're jest bottles, but Mr. C says he thinks they're treasures!" The boy's eyes were shining. He pointed with his shovel to three dirty glass bottles laid out on a bench.

"Cliffie did it!" said Mr. C, beaming. "He was helping me dig a hole to plant a camellia in memory of my wife—a *Methotiana rubra,* the old-fashioned kind that she liked best—and his spade hit something—"

"It clinked!" said the boy.

"And he had the good sense not to bang his spade on it and break it," said Mr. C. "He called me, and we dug carefully and got the bottle out, and then we went a little further and found two more!"

"Jest *layin'* there," the boy said. "Look at 'em, Miss Hattie! But be careful!"

"They're jest bottles," Cliffie said, "but Mr. C says
he thinks they're treasures!"

I picked up one of the bottles. It was a half-pint size, and the glass was a pretty, soft shade of green. Mr. C had wiped some of the dirt off with his handkerchief, and I could see a palmetto tree embossed on the side, with three words in a circle around it: "South-Carolina Dispensary."

"Oh!" I said, a light dawning. "This is one of those old, old whiskey bottles I've heard about—"

"Right!" said Mr. C excitedly, "from the time a hundred years ago when this state did its own bottling and selling of liquor! It was one of old Governor Ben 'Pitchfork' Tillman's schemes to make money, but it failed after just a few years. The scheme didn't last, but the bottles did—and they're valuable.... And look here, Miss Hattie, he found three sizes: a pint, a half-pint, and a puny one!"

Cliffie picked up the tiny two-ounce bottle carefully. "It's *cute*," he said, and held it up for me to see. It had the word "Souvenir" at the top and then: "S.C.I. and W.I. Exposition Charleston, S.C., 1901–2."

"Do you know anything about the Charleston Exposition, Mr. C?" I asked.

"I remember hearing my parents talk about it. They lived in Charleston then, and they remembered the hullabaloo. It was held in a place now called Hampton Park."

"What do the letters stand for?"

"I believe it was the South Carolina Interstate and West Indian Exposition. These must have been commemorative bottles, given out free."

He was all aglow with the find. "I'm going inside to find a box and some soft paper. I know a man at the Charleston Museum who can put a value on them." He put out his hand and Cliffie took it eagerly. "Son, we might be rich!"

It was hard to tell which one was the more excited.

What a lucky "dig"!

I walked home thinking about a short story I had read, years 'n' years ago, by DuBose Heyward, called "The Half-Pint Flask." It was about a New York man visiting a South Carolina plantation, and seeing graves in the Negro burying plot bordered with bottles. He was a connoisseur of bottles, and spied one so rare that he couldn't stand it. He slipped back at night and stole the bottle, much to his later sorrow. I *think* it was a South Carolina Dispensary bottle, but I'm not sure. I must find that story…. Anyway, these bottles didn't come from a grave. They're not "ha'nted."

September 15th

I didn't think my eyesight could get much worse, but it has deteriorated in recent days. I can't even see to make up my face. I put on lipstick by dead reckoning!

Today, as I was taking Louly a vase of zinnias from the Butterfly Garden, I walked through B Hall. One of the carts that the cleaning staff use to hold their supplies was sitting in the hall. A mop was sticking up out of it. To my poor eyes the mop head looked like a person, so I said "Good morning." The housekeeper heard me, and she couldn't help laughing. Then she saw my dismay, and was sorry. "Don't mind, honey," she said, "you was jest bein' polite."

Oh, me. When you start speaking to mops, it's *bad*.

～

Overheard:

I've always had a good memory. You might even call it a photographic memory...but I don't know...lately I seem to be running out of film....

September 16th

Mr. Cruickshank has washed the three discovered bottles carefully and put them on display in the lobby, on a shelf, behind glass. (He didn't trust old people picking them up.) He made a small sign to go underneath that reads:

These South Carolina Dispensary
bottles were unearthed by Master
Clifton S. Priest on FairAcres
grounds on Sept. 12, 1998.

Arthur and Dolly are so pleased, and Clifton is going around beaming. He is the envy of his brothers and sister.

September 18th

Last night I remembered my Cousin Boo, and thought of another of her many malapropisms. She was talking about her local baker. "Sometimes his bread is good, and sometimes it's not. He's very erotic."

Later

The secretary in the front office here, Nan Graves, is a love. She puts up with the "inmates" in an amazingly patient fashion. Sometimes three people are after her at once, while she's trying to answer the phone politely. She wraps packages, answers the intercom, and looks up phone numbers, addresses, and zip codes at the same time, without losing her "cool."

I've often thought that I would undoubtedly shoot two or three people before 10 A.M., if I had her job.

Today I went into her office to get some stamps. Geneva Tinken was just leaving, saying, "Well, I guess I'd better go get that done."

Several people were ahead of me, so I had to wait about ten minutes to make my purchase. Just as I was paying Nan for the stamps, her phone rang. She answered and listened patiently to the person on the line. After a minute she said, "Miss Geneva, I believe you said you had to go to your room and wash some underclothes.... Yes, ma'am.... You're welcome."

Nan hung up and grinned at me. "She wanted me to tell her what she had gone home to do!"

We had a good laugh. Maybe Nan is the one who should be keeping a diary.

September 21st

Some people here (not very many, thank goodness) seem to be obsessed with the number of hours that they sleep.

At breakfast you hear:

"I'll bet I didn't sleep six hours last night."

"I didn't close my eyes till after three o'clock."

"I rolled and tossed and finally got up and made a sandwich."

"I counted sheep until the sheep gave out, and so did I."

I think they forget about those two-hour afternoon naps; even one-hour midmorning naps, sometimes.

I want to tell them that my doctor says we don't *need* more than six hours sleep a night, at our age. I want to tell them to read, or watch late-night TV, and stop worrying about it.

Maybe it would be good if we had a "Sleep Chart" on the wall of Main Hall, where those who wanted to could write down the number of hours they had slept—making it a kind of official report, and (I hope) doing away with the necessity of talking about it!

September 25th

Mr. Cruickshank didn't stop with displaying the bottles at The Home. It turns out that he got in touch with museums in Charleston and Columbia. I ran into Mr. C at the mailboxes today, and he told me that one of the curators, who was a fancier of old bottles, called him up. He has a book about these South Carolina Dispensary bottles.

"Miss Hattie, he made me describe them in *detail*. He even asked if the half-pint bottle is green (it is) and if there's a hyphen between 'South' and 'Carolina'! And there is! That makes it more valuable! Fewer of those have been found.

"But Miss Hattie, the *real* find is the little bitty two-ounce souvenir bottle, made for that big exposition in Charleston in 1901. I'm not sure, but I think some big shots decided that whiskey, even in a cute bottle, was not a real good memento of our state, so they ordered the bottles destroyed. But a few had already been given away, and this is one of 'em! I hear it's worth a lot of money."

"Do you plan to sell them?"

"Oh, yes. And you know what I'm going to do with the money, Miss Hattie?" He leaned in close with a radiant smile. "Start a savings account for college expenses for Clifton and his siblings. With three kids of their own and two adopted ones, Arthur and Dolly can't possibly afford college for them all."

I told him what a wonderful idea that was. And I thought to myself that there will probably be others here who will be interested in contributing to such a fund. I parted from Mr. Cruickshank with renewed faith in people.

October 1

Big news, Dear Diary, about the "Treasure of Cruickshank Cottage."

As it turned out, Mr. C learned about a wealthy bottle collector in Virginia, called him up, described the bottles, and sold them to him for a sum that staggered me. (I'm not used to what collectors pay, today, for things they want.) The Priest children have their own savings account now, I understand. Mr. C added some funds of his own, and a number of us contributed to the project. It has been a joy to see a poor, utterly desolate human being take on new life and change into a useful person, all because of an innocent, endearing small boy. "And a little child shall lead them...."

7

Memory Lane

October 3rd

I sat down by Esther on a sofa in the lobby. She was looking at the morning paper.

"I declare," she said. "These obituaries kill me. Here's one about a fellow I used to know: Fred Linkletter. He worked for my Charlie. Fred had the misfortune to fall in love with a woman who was his inferior in every way when it came to character. It says here, 'Survived by his beloved wife Arline.' *Beloved!* He had to throw her out twice that I know of. He finally let her come back because she didn't have anywhere else to go. '…and by his beloved daughter Patricia.' Hummph! She was as no-count as her mama. Pat shot Fred twice…I mean on two

separate occasions. She was a poor shot, thank goodness, and the bullet just grazed an arm or a leg, or something, but she really tried to do away with her 'beloved'
daddy. It says, 'The family will receive mourners after the
service at 112 Union St.' Oh boy! That'll be a wingding.
I expect those two females will be having more of a
'Whoopee-the-Old-Goat's-Gone' party."

I walked away feeling a little bit upset. I'd rather think
the "Old Goat" was beloved by *some*body.

October 4th

Last night I lay in bed remembering a story my
mother told me, about something that really happened
in her hometown in Alabama, years 'n' years ago. I think
it was the use of the word "inferior" that made the story
linger in my mind all this time.

Many people in the small town, especially those of the
female variety, were looking forward to the marriage of
Miss Nettie Saunders to Mr. Walter Canterbury. Nearly
twenty-five years had passed since Appomattox and the
end of the War Between the States, but there was still little money in the South to be spent on entertainment; so
a large evening wedding, with reception to follow at the
home of the bride, was an event to anticipate.

But about midafternoon of the wedding day, when
the ladies were busy turning up their front bangs in

tight rolls on "curl rags," or putting buttermilk masks on their faces, or hanging their men's best suits on the line for airing and brushing, there went from back door to back door, all over town, a small boy. He bore a handwritten missive which stated that there would be no wedding, because Miss Nettie had run off that morning and married Mr. Harold Meadows. However, since the newlyweds had now returned, the reception would take place as scheduled.

Now there was *real* anticipation. Even those husbands who had been lukewarm (not being overly fond of standing around eating dainty sandwiches and listening to chitchat) were filled with curiosity. They wondered how the brazen couple would act, and whether or not Walter, the poor spurned bridegroom, would dare to put in an appearance.

Surprisingly, he did. Mama said that a complete hush fell on everyone in the Saunders's front parlor when Walter, wearing his wedding finery, entered and went down the receiving line. When he got to the bride, dazzling in her nuptial gown of white satin and lace ("No use to waste it," she had decided), he stopped, looked in her eyes, and asked her, "Miss Nettie, how could you do me so?"

It was said that she looked at her feet, and made no answer. This was high drama, and the story was told and re-told in the town for decades. There was no fight between the winning bridegroom and the losing one. In fact, the bride's mother was determined that her stellar entertainment would not be spoiled by a little thing like a switch in the cast of characters.

Being a lady given to the use and mis-use of such ten-dollar words as "immaterial," she flitted from group to group, saying, "Come on, now, everybody. Eat, drink, and dance. Don't be downhearted. *I'm* not. It's inferior to me *which* man Nettie married!"

October 6th

Some of us were sitting on the porch after supper tonight, enjoying the quiet ending of the day. Mr. Cruickshank came out, and we welcomed him warmly. He smiled, and sat down. Such a metamorphosis!

"Dug up anything good lately, Mr. C?" one of the men asked.

"No, but I think I'll put in some more camellias. So who knows?" he asked, smiling.

There followed some small talk about things people in the South had unearthed.

"My great-uncle dug up a tin box full of Confederate money up near Columbia," said Graham. "I guess somebody buried it when Sherman's army was bearin' down, and never came back for it—maybe because the whole box full wasn't worth more'n five dollars."

Somebody piped up with, "Save your Confederate money, son. The South's gonna rise again!" That brought a good laugh.

"I found a lady's wedding ring in the sand on the beach at the Isle of Palms once," said Curtis. "It had some initials and a date inside, so I described it in a newspaper ad, and a lady with those initials came right around to claim it. Happiest lady you ever saw. That made me feel *good.*"

Curtis looked wistful. "I was only about seventeen, and still had some romance in my soul."

"Did she kiss you, Curt?" Bill asked.

"That she did!" he said, smiling. "Nice-looking lady, too. Not a day over thirty-five." He chuckled, and so did we.

"I'll tell you what I wish you and Cliffie could've found, Mr. C," said Bill. "A slave tag! They bring a *lot* of money. Into the thousands!"

Mr. Cruickshank looked thoughtful. "I don't know about that," he said. "I would have had trouble explaining to Cliffie what it was…what it was used for."

"What are you-all talkin' about?" asked Lily.

"About a metal tag that some male slaves had to wear on a chain around their necks," explained Bill. "I understand the tag bore a number, not a name, and gave the slave's occupation, such as 'Blacksmith,' or 'Cobbler,' and so forth. Not many of them have been found—

I suppose because they were usually buried with the slave."

"I can see your point, Mr. C," said Curtis, speaking slowly. "It would be hard for a child, today, to take in the fact that human beings were owned by other human beings…in *America*…in the nineteenth century!"

We sat quietly for several minutes. Some of the older people in my family had spoken of slavery as a "necessary evil"—necessary to produce the crops that the country needed before mechanical devices came about. Still, the thought of people owning people is not a happy one.

I decided I was glad, too, that Mr. C and his little friend had not dug up a slave tag. Much better to find bottles—even whiskey bottles!

October 7th

Almost everybody here can lay claim to one or more Confederate soldiers in their backgrounds. (There are two or three among us who could claim Yankee-soldier forebears, but they keep pretty quiet.)

Ethel talks a lot about her great-grandfather General Luther K. Armstrong. I don't say anything. I don't dare tell her what I've heard all my life about General Armstrong. The story goes that General Armstrong rode up to his men, who were hiding behind trees from the nearby Yankees, and uttered these memorable *last* words: "Don't worry, boys, those Yanks couldn't hit the side of a barn at this dis—"

October 9th

This notice appeared in *Family Affairs,* The Home's newsletter, last week:

> The Program Department has received a request from Miss Felicia McNaughton, who is a student in History at the College of Charleston.
>
> Miss McNaughton is working on an oral history project about "The Depression Years and World War II: Their Effect on Southern Living." She feels that she could glean a great deal from the memories of people at this Home.
>
> If you are willing to share your memories with this student, please come to the library at 3 P.M. on Thursday.

About thirty people—mostly women—showed up. The girl was so attractive and so grateful to us for coming out, that we found it easy to open up to her. She explained that she would be recording the meeting on her tape recorder and asked if any of us would be uncomfortable being taped. We shook our heads. It would take more than that to daunt us.

Felicia got us started by telling about her grandmother, whose father—like millions of others—lost his
job in 1930. There was no breadwinner, no money for
food. "My grandmother," said Felicia, "who had been
raised in luxury, had to leave boarding school, come
home, and go to work as a clerk in the dime store, so
that her family could eat! It was her story that
prompted this project of mine. Did any of you have a
similar experience?"

We looked at each other. To my surprise, Grace
Newcomb, usually very quiet, spoke up. Grace always
dresses beautifully, and wears gorgeous diamonds. I
think her late husband had been "well off."

"The Depression hit just when I was going off to college," she began. "I offered to stay home and try to find
a job, but my parents were adamant. I must get that
degree, and be the teacher I had always wanted to be.
But, oh, it was hard...." she hesitated. "This will give
you an idea. Winthrop College at that time showed a
movie for the students every Saturday afternoon; but it
cost a dime to get in, and I never had a dime. I didn't
have *any* spending money. I could barely buy the necessary textbooks.

"My father died; and how my mother managed to put
all four of us through Winthrop and Clemson—even
though they were 'state schools'—I will never know.

"Once in a great while my older brother, who had finished Clemson and gotten a WPA job, would write to me and enclose a dollar. That dollar bill was a beautiful sight to me! I could go to a movie or two, and get a candy bar, and buy some stamps!"

Felicia was listening avidly. "Did you graduate?" she asked.

"'Deed I did! And got a good teaching job. Things were never that bad again; but I can't forget how rough it was, and I sometimes wonder if today's young people would endure such hardships."

"I don't think they could," spoke up Cecil. "They're too soft. Oh—" he caught himself. "Present company excepted.... Oh, Grace, speaking of your teaching job, I'll bet you made all of sixty dollars a month."

"That's what I made, exactly," she answered. "It seemed like a fortune. I was luckier than some of my classmates who got teaching jobs in small towns that had to pay them in what was called scrip. Those pieces of paper were worthless at the time, but I think they eventually paid off."

"I remember my mother 'turning' my father's shirt collars," said Eloise. "She'd take the collar off when it got frayed at the top, turn it over, and sew it back on."

"One thing I remember," said Fred, "was worrying about my shoes when they'd begin to feel thin on the bottom. I would cut a piece of cardboard and stick it in the shoes. Half-soling cost two dollars, and two dollars was a lot of money."

"I remember when shoes were rationed—and butter and eggs and coffee," said Augusta.

"Oh, come on, Gusta. You're getting the Depression and World War II mixed up."

"That's all right," said our college student, "I want to hear those memories, too."

"That was terrible having shoes rationed," said Grace. "We had four kids. All the ration stamps had to go for their growing feet. Tom and I didn't get a new pair of shoes till long after the war was over, when they were finally available again."

"Do you-all remember how we saved tin cans during the war?" somebody asked.

"*I* do," said Harriet. "I was in charge of collecting them, from all over town. We'd tell people to cut the bottom out of an empty can, then mash the can flat. They'd put bags of these flattened cans out in front of their houses, and I'd arrange for trucks to pick them up. Then they were sent off somewhere, to be melted down—"

"I remember white margarine," broke in Gusta.

"I do, too," I said. "I remember asking one of my children to help out by coloring the oleo. The store would give you a little bag of orange coloring, remember? But my child got tired of mixing the coloring in, and said, 'Mama, why can't we just eat *clean* butter?'"

"Do you remember 'Meatless Tuesdays'?" somebody asked.

"Oh, yes," said Grace. "And I remember gasoline being rationed, so we had to walk a lot. Did us good."

"Young lady," Cecil said to Felicia, "you may get the impression that all we were concerned about during the war were our inconveniences. It was not so. I was tremendously impressed by the way this *entire* country came forward, with *every*body straining to help the War Effort. It was phenomenal—and heartening.... I wonder if it could happen now?"

Two or three people shook their heads; then some-body said, "Well, as hard as the war years were, I think the Depression years were worse. To me it's a sad, terri-bly gray area in our history."

"It was *that*," said Harriet. "But do you know some-thing? I've thought many times lately that a small depression might be good for this country. It might help us get our values straightened out."

The meeting broke up, with Felicia thanking us pro-fusely for helping her. We told her we were glad of a chance to dredge up old memories and comment on them—especially when somebody really *wanted* to hear what we had to say. We wished her a happy A+ on her project.

8

Small Blessings

October 10th

I give everybody notice: "If you come to see me, these days, you're going to have to thread some needles!"

I can still see to do very easy things, like tacking up a loose hem; but I can't see that infinitesimal hole in the needle. I stab at it and stab at it, and give up in frustration. The pesky thread goes to one side of the needle or the other, but never *through.*

So a visitor sits with my sewing basket resting on his or her lap, and while we chatter, he or she threads me up a goodly supply of needles, mostly in white thread. Not a soul has demurred. I believe people are glad to be told small ways in which they can help one another.

One of the worst things about this near-blindness is not being able to see spots on my clothes. I've alerted my friends, asking them to please check me; but some of them are reluctant. I wish they'd say, "You were careless with the crumbs yesterday, old girl. Go home and change." That would be the better part of friendship.

Later

I belong to the Drayton Presbyterian Church, and had to have my picture taken last week for the church directory. Oh, groan.

When I got there I was dismayed to find I had not put on any earrings. The photographer's assistant offered me hers, but they were for pierced ears. My lobes felt curiously naked without their pearls. Now I await the results. Will my large lobes look exceedingly bare? Will I look kind of undressed? Will anybody in the wide world *care?*

~

A memory:

I'm thinking about a long-ago Sunday.

Our minister was on the porch of the church, in his black robe, greeting the people as they came out of the sanctuary.

I was in the car, rounding up my brood. One was missing.

"Does anybody know where Nancy is?" I asked.

"I do," said Ray, aged five.

"Where?"

"She's up there on the porch, talking to God."

October 12th

Coming out of the dining room today I was behind a man and woman who were holding hands.

"I always love to see a couple holding hands," I said pleasantly.

"Don't get excited," the man said to me dryly. "We're just holding each other up."

October 15th

I think it was in the musical *Oklahoma!* that there was a song called "Everything's Up to Date in Kansas City." Well, Dear Diary, FairAcres can boast of being up to date, also. Yesterday, our pool was opened for business, complete with a warm, soothing Jacuzzi section. Paul consulted with the physical therapy department and added this feature to comfort aching, arthritic joints. I am looking forward to trying it.

In another modern twist, Internet jokes have infiltrated The Home! A friend who has fun with his computer sent me some T-shirt slogans that have been floating around on the Internet:

"I want it all, and I want it delivered."

"Filthy, stinking rich.... Well, two out of three ain't bad."

"That's it! I'm calling Grandma!"

"Wrinkled was not one of the things I wanted to be when I grew up."

"Procrastinate now!"

He also sent me a list of definitions that someone "e-mailed" to him:

Flatulence: The emergency vehicle that picks you up after you are run over by a steamroller.

Rectitude: The formal, dignified demeanor assumed by a proctologist just before he examines you.

Flabbergasted: Appalled at how much weight you have gained.

Coffee: A person who is coughed upon.

And my personal favorite:

Macadam: The first man on Earth...according to the Scottish Bible.

October 19th

Somebody gave me what they called a "Chinese back-scratcher" last Christmas. I doubt that it cost more than three dollars—and I wouldn't take ten times that much for it. It's one of those small things that make the world a more comfortable place, and make you wonder how you got along without it.

The little scratcher not only causes me to go "Aaaah" when it reaches and relieves itching spots on my person, but it also serves to rake things out from hard-to-reach places, under and behind large pieces of furniture.

Blessings on the Chinese for inventing it, and on my friend for procuring and presenting to me a small gadget that gives large returns.

As the years roll on, many things get harder and harder to accomplish, such as: filing the nails on my right hand; pulling up a long zipper in the back of a dress; bending my bad knees enough to step into panties; reading the ridiculously small numbers in the phone book; waiting for a boring person to come to the end of a long, boring account.

John Dryden told us to "possess our souls with patience...." As my soul ages, patience seems harder and harder to possess.

October 21st

There are kitchenettes on each floor of the Main Building here, for the use of people who have only one room, not an apartment.

Somebody keeps the coffeemaker filled all the time in the D-Hall kitchenette. It always smells good, and anyone is welcome to a cup.

I was there this morning, pouring myself a "cuppa," when Gusta came in. She was holding a small covered dish.

"Somebody's always helpin' themselves to whatever I leave in this fridge," she said, "even when it has my name on it." And then she grinned. "I fixed 'em this time," she said. "They won't steal this cheese casserole I brought home from the dining room today." She showed me the top of the dish. She had taped a note to it, bearing her name "Augusta Barton," and saying, "This is already ten days old."

That Gusta!

October 25th

The daughter of a beloved couple here was visiting them over the weekend, and last night she sang old songs for us in the dining room after supper.

What a *treat!*

She made us believe there really *is* a "balm in Gilead"; and there was a tear on many an elderly cheek when she sang, "sometimes I feel like a motherless child, a long way f'um home."

For depth of feeling, and simple beauty, it's hard to beat a good, well-sung spiritual.

9

Ill Wind

November 2nd

Two nights ago—on Halloween!—one of the big
Atlantic storms that hit our beautiful Lowcountry from
time to time swept through Drayton. Thankfully, this
one remained a Tropical Storm and did not strike us
with the full force of a hurricane, as did "Hugo" in 1989.
I could tell you some stories about *that*.

We were safe and dry at The Home this time, but
some of Drayton's citizens were not so lucky. A number
of homes were extensively damaged, and people had to
seek shelter in the activities building of one of the local
churches. (Oh, how well we remember our single night

of inconvenience last summer when we were evacuated because of the tanker-truck crash!)

One of the majestic old live oaks downtown succumbed to the force of the winds, slightly damaging the elementary school. And not too far away, one of Drayton's treasures, a lovely Azalea Park, was severely battered. There are already plans, spearheaded by the local Jaycees, I believe, for a community campaign to help those in need and to restore the park.

Retta and Sidney Metcalf sent out a notice today that a number of Meals-on-Wheels recipients were affected. I feel a mobilization coming on among the caring people here. Really, I do feel fortunate to be surrounded by such wonderful neighbors. We have our share of "characters," who can "try men's (and women's) souls," but FairAcres is blessed with many willing hands and generous hearts.

Thank goodness Sidney and Retta's cruise took place a few weeks ago and was free of stormy weather.

November 3rd

I went to check on Louly today, and found Arthur there by her bed, holding her hand, like a son. She looks so frail now, but she was beaming on Arthur like a proud mother.

"But *your* house," she was saying, "how did it fare in the storm?"

"Kudzu Kottage came through fine," he said. "Lost a few shingles over the porch, and I've already replaced 'em. Oh! There were three baskets in the backyard that the boys put vegetables in when they're pickin'." Artie found 'em two blocks away, perched up in a tree, not even damaged! There was a lotta wind in that storm."

"I'll bet he was proud of himself," said Louly.

"Yes, ma'am," said Arthur. "Then he and I went to check on Mr. Stringfellow's little house. You know I keep an eye on it since he has been in the hospital down in Charleston," he added. "A big limb was across the front steps to the porch, but Artie and I got that cleaned up, and there was no other damage."

Mr. Ben Stringfellow is the nice man who used to come out to sing for us and play his guitar. I knew that the old gentleman's health had gone down a lot this year, and that he had been receiving treatment at the Veterans Administration Hospital.

"I hate to tell you," said Arthur, "but I don't really think he'll be able to come back and live on his own."

This was sad news. We all liked the dear, good-natured man, who knew and sang the *best* old songs.

"I'll tell you what I'll do, Arthur," I said, "I'll write a letter to Mr. Stringfellow and get a lot of our people to sign it. Perhaps Artie and the children can add some 'Get Well' drawings, and we'll send him everything."

"That's a great idea," Arthur said. "And I'll bet Miss Cora would make him some of her tea cakes."

Arthur and I left together, and as we walked out of the Health Center, we talked about Louly. Although her mind has not been terribly affected by the stroke, it has become obvious to us that she is failing physically. I expect she will continue to need skilled nursing care and will not be able to return to her apartment. The sadness of her situation is much ameliorated by wonderful nurses and the joy and comfort of her relationship with the Priest family.

November 4th

Some of our nicest residents come from the town of Drayton. They're lucky, because their friends and relatives can come frequently to see them.

Susie Fleming is one of them. Her son Henry came out to have dinner with her and talk about the storm damage. Afterwards he corralled some of us at nearby tables.

"Would you folks give me a minute?" he asked. He's so pleasant, we would have given him an hour. "I'm an officer in the Jaycees, and we're getting ready to put on a variety show at the Drayton Theater on Main Street. It's to raise money to replant the park and help with various other projects.

"We need more people to volunteer for the show. I'll bet there's a lot of talent here. I wonder if we could count on you people for one or two acts in the variety show?"

There was quiet for a minute. We looked at each other. Finally Bill Nixon (bless his heart; he always comes through) said, "Maybe we could get up a kitchen band. You know, one with washboards and kettles and kazoos, and crazy things. The noise is horrible, but it's a lot of fun. I was in one, once."

"That sounds *perfect!*" cried Henry Fleming. "We haven't had one here—the folks would *love* it. Would you organize that, Mr. Nixon?"

Bill looked around. "Will you-all help me?"

We all said we would. Paul said, "I'll make a fool of myself for you, Bill, and for the Jaycees. I'll be a band member; but I'm sitting here wondering where in the world we're going to find a washboard, in this day and time? And a metal thimble to strum it with?"

November 7th

We started right away gathering materials for the band. Some of them were easy to find: a cluster of measuring spoons to rattle, a frying pan to hit with a big spoon, an old banjo, even a big jug; but as Paul predicted, we were defeated when it came to finding a washboard.

We rummaged through all the hardware stores in the vicinity to no avail. Most of the clerks didn't even know what a washboard looked like.

Not only that. We were also stymied when we tried to locate a metal thimble. We were told that in order to get the most agonized sound from a washboard, it must be "played" by strumming its metal face with a metal thimble. Alas, we found that the few thimbles being made today are all plastic. Some of the ladies at The Home have a treasured gold or silver thimble that belonged to a beloved grandmother, but they do not care to have it scraped against a washboard.

Knowing that ours would not be a real kitchen band without the missing ingredients, Cora and I decided today that we would scour the countryside. (We don't have much else to do, goodness knows.) Cora is lucky to still have her "wheels." She said her car battery needed charging, so we set off, taking a country road toward Moncks Corner.

We had no luck at our first several stops. Either no one was at home or the inhabitant just laughed and shook her head when we revealed the object of our search.

Eventually we had a piece of luck. An attractive young couple who are renovating a farmhouse told us about nearby neighbors who still have a barn on their property. The barn has become a catchall for many old farming implements and such.

Following their directions, we came to a small house that had a large barn down a second road a good way from the house. Cora looked at me, and I nodded. We took the second road, parked on the side of the barn away from the house, and got out. I peeked into the old building through a crack. "Cora, you won't believe it!" I whispered. "There's one hanging on a nail. A *wash*board!"

You would have thought we had found a diamond bracelet. Grinning like two mischievous little girls, we retraced our path and headed toward the house. A nice-looking woman in a large apron answered our knock. We told her that we wanted to buy a washboard. She looked puzzled.

"Do you use it anymore?" I asked.

"No. I have a washing machine. I had forgotten that old thing was still hanging out there...."

"Would you please sell it to us?"

She looked uncertain.

"We'll give you ten dollars for it," I said, wanting to offer the woman a fair price. Her eyebrows went up in astonishment.

I had an idea. "You could give the money to your church, maybe."

Her frown disappeared. "Yes, I could do that."

I explained our involvement in the kitchen band for the Jaycees program, and then I had another brainstorm. "Would you happen to have a thimble we could buy?"

"A *thimble?* Why, yes, I've got two of 'em. Mine and Mama's."

"Would you sell one to me for ten dollars?"

"Well, Mama's is silver, and I wouldn't want to part with it. But mine came from the dime store—I expect it's tin or some such metal. I reckon I really don't have need of two."

She went in the house and found the thimble. Then she went with us to the barn and lifted the washboard from the wall. We paid her, thanked her profusely, and drove off, leaving the woman watching our departure with a slightly dazed expression on her face.

We laughed as we talked about our day of searching.

Cora said, "You know something, Hattie? I'll bet I can tell you what takes place around at least one supper table tonight. I'll bet someone we talked to today will say, 'Honey, you wouldn't believe what happened to me today. Two old ladies came by tryin' to find a washboard and a thimble. Those poor old souls from that Home hafta sew up their own clothes, and that's not all! They hafta scrub 'em on a washboard!'"

*She went with us to the barn and lifted the
washboard from the wall.*

We laughed until Cora nearly ran the car off the road. We were out twenty dollars, but it had been a great day. We returned just in time for supper and proudly presented our treasures to Bill Nixon.

10

What Goes Around...

November 8th

Tonight I sat at my beautiful desk that Amanda Pate's father made. I wrote a newsy letter to send to Mr. Stringfellow from his friends at The Home.

Then I re-read the most recent letter I had from Amanda. In her new life in High Point, which she seems to like more and more, I'm glad she continues to find time for an occasional note to me. It's interesting to see her handwriting and her choice of words get more mature; but I want to say to that dear child: Please don't grow up too fast!

I've been thinking about Amanda because her old teacher, Mrs. Trotter, called this week and asked me to read a story to the children the night of the Jaycees' program. (I met the teacher last year when Amanda invited me to come to school to talk to her class about my books.) I tried to wiggle out of it politely, but she promised to see to all the arrangements, and it was impossible to say "No." I'm flattered, but oh, what have I gotten myself into?!

November 9th

I went to the HCC to visit Louly today. Her door was slightly ajar, and I peeped in. Arthur Priest was sitting by her bed, reading the newspaper to her. (This is Saturday, his day off.)

How fitting, I thought. She had taught him to read, and now, with her eyesight failing (and her mind, a little) he was giving her pleasure by relating Dennis the Menace's devilment to her. *What goes around comes around,* I said to myself, when things work out as they should.

I slipped away, deciding not to interrupt their togetherness, which pleased me no end. I went back after supper when she was alone.

November 10th

For several days FairAcres Home has been alive with "The Sound of Music"—but not the kind of pleasing melodies that emanated from that wonderful movie.

What it is, is cacophony. Our kitchen band practiced yesterday in the dining room after lunch. Yes, Dear Diary, I said "our." Cora and I decided we'd rather be in it than to listen to it.

Some stragglers sitting at tables near the back listened for a few minutes, their legs jerking with the strength of the rhythm. We *do* have rhythm, if nothing else. But I guess our "music" was too much for them, because it wasn't long before they hurried out, holding their hands over their ears.

There's a piano at the theater and one to practice on here. Paul picks out chords on the twangy banjo while the piano carries the "melody," if the hideous sound can be called that.

Sidney beats the back of a frying pan with a large spoon, and somebody rattles dried black-eyed peas in tin cans. Curtis made what's called a "gut bucket" with a washtub and a broom handle, which Lily plunks away on. Curtis himself, it turns out, actually plays the harmonica.

Wearing a chef's hat borrowed from the kitchen, I alternate between the piano and "conducting" with a wooden spoon. Bill adds a breathy note, blowing into the mouth of a jug. Oh, and of course the hard-won washboard is being scraped savagely by Cora with the "antique" thimble.

Cecil is upset. He wanted to play Second Washboard, but there's "no such animal"; so if he joins us he will have to settle for Second Frying Pan.

We're looking for a name for the group. I think it should be called "An End to Music As We Know It."

November 11th

Today we had corned beef and cabbage for lunch—not my favorite menu, but I was glad I went because of what I heard. Emily McKnight was in rare form.

Emily is partial to a glass of cool chardonnay before lunch, which is fine with me. In fact, The Home's doctor recommends wine before meals, to increase our appetites and to soothe our aging nerves.

Today I think Emily had been "partial" to two or three glasses of chardonnay. She rattled on, amusingly. She had brought a story, found among her treasures, that her grandson, Larry, had written when he was about nine years old and in the fourth grade. Emily explained to us that his teacher, Miss Spencer, was determined to increase the children's vocabularies. Every day she would put three new, unusual words on the blackboard for the pupils to use in sentences.

On this particular day, one of the words was "frugal."

"Miss Spencer," asked Larry, "what does 'frugal' mean?"

"It means 'saving...to save.' Larry, can you put it into a sentence?"

"'To save'? Sure!" After a pause he said, "Sure, Miss Spencer, I can write you a *story* about that!"

"Fine, Larry."

Here is what he had written (I borrowed the story and made a copy):

Once upon a time there was a night in shining armer.

He had a lady fare.

One day the lady fare was riding her horse. The horse bucked and through her into a deep ditch.

"Frugal me! Frugal me!" yelled the lady fare.

Jest then the night in shining armer came along.

He frugalled her. They got married and lived happy ever after.

The End

I ask you, Dear Diary, wasn't that a good tale to hear on a dull, rainy day?

Thank you, Lord, for people like Emily. There are so many of them here!

And while I'm in a grateful mood, I will bless my Sam, for working hard and making wise investments that make it possible for me to be in this great place. I wish he had lived to enjoy it with me.... I wish I could have "frugalled" him!

November 12th

Emily's story yesterday reminded me of Cousin Boo and her mixed-up phrases:

"I don't want any more kittens, so I had my cat spaded."

Other malapropisms I've heard:

"Let's let that lie dominant."

"That's good public elations."

Woman (to her child dawdling behind, in the store): "Come on! Don't dwaddle!"

"In the nick-up of time."

"I like that piece, 'Rhap-*sod*-dy in Blue.'"

"Don't you come in here spouting a lot of wild acquisitions!"

"He's well off. He's got a very ludicrous business."

Mark Twain said, "The difference between the almost-right word and the right word is really a large matter—'tis the difference between the lightning bug and the lightning."

Whew!

Maybe I should deliberate a moment longer, before letting my flighty pen accost the clean, white, innocent paper....

~

Overheard:
She's sick in bed with the doctor.

November 13th (Friday the 13th)

For my story-reading part of the Jaycees' evening, I have arranged to have my own reading lamp, the wonderful one that bends over my shoulder and not only illuminates but magnifies.

A parent from the school is going to transport the lamp, as well as my favorite rocking chair and a small oriental rug I have in the front hall, over to the theater in his van. He will arrange it all at the appropriate time to make a little scene for my "Story Time" act.

Then he will get it all back to me afterward! The organizers are keeping their promise to make this venture as easy for me as possible.

I have considered several stories. One that occurred to me today—this Friday the thirteenth—was "The Legend of Sleepy Hollow" by Washington Irving. Ichabod Crane and his encounter with the Headless Horseman seemed particularly appropriate in response to the storm that occurred on Halloween night! But I think my audience will be too young for such a spooky story.

Instead, my choice is out of a favorite book from my own childhood. I'm going to read a short trio of the Uncle Remus tales by Joel Chandler Harris: "Uncle Remus Initiates the Little Boy," "The Wonderful Tar-Baby Story," and "How Mr. Rabbit Was Too Sharp for Mr. Fox."

I am to read to the children just after the community supper, while arrangements are set in place for the evening's entertainment. I must get in a nice, long afternoon nap!

11

Show Time

November 16th

The big night of the "Jaycees Jollification" came last night, and I believe it went very well, Dear Diary.

There must have been about twenty children sitting around me to hear the stories of Brer Rabbit and Brer Fox. My listeners were wonderfully well behaved and reacted with laughter at the antics of these marvelous characters.

I had not really wanted to do the reading. I was in two other acts, and did not want to appear to be "hogging" the show; but the delighted giggles and whoops from the children—as the rabbit got himself stuck tighter and tighter to the tar-baby and then finally out-foxed Brer Fox—made me glad I had done it. Most of them had never heard these time-worn tales before!

Then I had to scurry backstage to join my confederates as the organizers had scheduled our kitchen band, which we had named the "Home Hooters," to play early. (Maybe they were afraid some of us might nod off or something if we waited too long.)

After a talented young duo from the high school performed "The Star Spangled Banner," the Jaycees' president gave us a grand intro, and we were well into "Alexander's Ragtime Band" when the curtain went up. Feet stomped and the building shook. Such scraping and rattling and banging had never been heard in this quiet theater before. Certain sounds seemed to stand out: the ugly, hollow *whump-whump* sound that Bill made as he blew into the empty whisky jug and the metallic scraping on the washboard.

The piano and harmonica carried the semblance of a tune; the rest was foot-stomping noise and rattling good fun. The audience loved it. I'm sure we were heard in Jedburg, four miles away.

Our second number was "Yes, Sir, That's My Baby," and we ended with, strangely enough, "The Missouri Waltz." I fear it was more of a rending than a rendition. Anyway, we got a big hand. Then four of our men went

The audience loved it. I'm sure we were heard in Jedburg, four miles away.

to the front—a barbershop quartet. They sang two oldies: "Alabamy Bound" and "Bye-Bye, Blackbird."

Then they launched into that old jazzy number that starts:

I'll be down to get you in a taxi, Honey.
You'd better be ready 'bout hap-past eight.

At the end of that, they asked Marcia and me to come up and join them in singing a song I had written called "The End-of-the-Century Blues." I'm not going to quote it here. It's too corny. I wrote it in too big a hurry; but I did manage to bring out the thought that the twentieth has been *our* century—from "Ja-da, Ja-da, Jing, Jing, Jing" to the "September Song," from "Over There" to "The Wild Blue Yonder," from "Casey at the Bat" to the Atlanta Braves. They gave us a standing ovation. Bless their kind hearts.

After that we could relax and enjoy seeing the Jaycees make nuts of themselves, in act after act, from seats they had saved for us down front.

I was glad to read on the program that Russell Culpepper would sing a solo. His bass voice is famous locally. I hoped he would perform that favorite of all *basso profundo* songs—and, lo and behold, he did!

Russell, a well-padded gentleman (as most good basses seem to be) was in full voice, and made the rafters ring. He had us all struggling with him and pulling for him when he got to the last line:

> Rocked
> in the
> *cray*-dul
> of
> the
> Deeeeeeep.

That "deep" was *down there*—I mean, *way* down. It rumbled and grumbled. His stomach shook a little, and I believe the floor rattled a little. It was *won*derful.

A *good* evening—and, I understand, a profitable one. What with the entrance fees and the auction of four paintings donated by local artists, a goodly sum was raised for a good cause.

November 19th

I get up every morning, dress myself, fix my breakfast (or go to the dining room, once in a blue moon), read the paper—and then I'm ready to go back to bed! Isn't that awful? Dear Diary, I'm ashamed to admit it, but it's true. That high, beautifully stuffed mattress looks so inviting. I tell myself, in a paraphrase of Mr. Longfellow: "Life is real, life is earnest, and the *bed* is not its goal," but that does no good. I can't resist. I take off my shoes and crawl back into bed fully clothed, yawning and luxuriating. Usually after just a few minutes I wake up, feeling sinfully relaxed.

I wonder if many other old critters have such an aberration? I'm ashamed to ask.

A friend recently sent me these observations on the "adventure" of growing old. They're too true for comfort.

Everything is farther away than it used to be. It is now twice as far to the corner, and they have added a hill.

I have given up running for the bus; it leaves earlier than it used to.

It seems to me they are making stairs steeper than in the old days. And have you noticed the smaller print they use in the newspapers?

There is no sense in asking anyone to read aloud any more, as everybody speaks in such a low voice I can hardly hear them.

The material in dresses is so skimpy now, especially around the hips and waist, that it is almost impossible to reach one's shoelaces. And the sizes don't run the way they used to, the 12's and 14's are so much smaller.

Even people are changing. They are so much younger than they used to be when I was their age. On the other hand, people my own age are so much older than I am.

I ran into an old classmate the other day, and she has aged so much that she did not recognize me. I got to thinking about the poor dear when I was combing my hair this morning, and I noticed my reflection in the mirror. They don't even make good mirrors like they used to.

November 20th

Geneva was coming down the hall today looking dejected. I thought it in order to express a little concern.

"Good morning, Geneva. I saw you in the doctor's waiting room yesterday. What's wrong?"

She drew herself up. "That's between my doctor, my God, and me," she pronounced, and stalked off.

Maybe I should be more chary with my concern.

Later

Overheard:

It's hard to be nostalgic when you can't remember anything!

And at the table tonight:

"Don't talk to me right now."

"Why not?"

"Because I'm chewing. When I'm chewing, my hearing aid doesn't work."

Speaking of hearing problems, Dear Diary, I think I will write to my congressman about something that drives me crazy. Heck, I think I'll write to my senator too!

I suppose the people I really should write to are the presidents of NBC and CBS and ABC, because the problem is the terrible, awful, overwhelming loudness of the background music on TV programs.

I hear complaints about it on all sides and from all ages, not just the elderly; although, of course, it's worse for those of us who are losing our hearing.

It seems to be a conspiracy. Just as the play is reaching a climax and you need to hear every word of every line to unravel the plot—that's when the so-called music crescendos. All loud pedals are pressed, all horns blare, all strings wail. It's seldom a pleasing sound; just maddeningly loud and obnoxious. The crucial lines are drowned out completely.

Why? What *is* the point?... If I were younger I would start a crusade.

We're entering a long, *long* season of listening to presidential candidates. I think I will write to every one of them. If one of them puts it in his platform—No More Loud Background Music—I will campaign for that gentleman (or lady).

November 21st

Today Esther drove some of us in her car to the Piggly-Wiggly to stock up on some delicious wickedness: soft drinks, candy, and cookies. We say the purchases are made "to have on hand just in case the grands come." But, the truth is, we grandmothers (and grandfathers, too) still enjoy these treats.

On the way, a hearse passed us, weaving in and out of traffic, fast.

"Pshaw me! Look at that!" said Esther. Then she looked up at us in the back, through her rearview mirror. "What are you-all giggling about? A speeding hearse is not funny."

"No, Esther: We're laughing at the expression you used."

"'Pshaw me'? What's funny about that?"

"Nothing, I suppose. We just never heard it before."

"My goodness! My grandmother said it all the time."

"Like mine used to say, 'Gracious peace!'" said Cora.

"And mine used to say, 'The law!' when she was surprised," I put in, "though I don't think it had anything to do with law. Maybe it came from 'The Lord help us!' or something."

"One of my mother's favorites was, 'Oh, for garden seed!'" said Marcia.

"I think I'll stick to 'pshaw me,' said Esther.

November 22nd

Several residents including yours truly have recently had to give up driving, and the editor of our weekly paper, *Family Affairs,* thought a bit of humor might be in order, so I wrote the following:

AN OLD LADY'S LAMENT

I've given my trusty "wheels" away,
And the public is delighted.
The carport sits there, bare, forlorn,
And I feel sad and slighted.

I wasn't *that* bad a driver, now!
Not like the *real* offenders.
I only caused two traffic jams
And had three fender benders.

It had to come; but oh, I grieve.
I've lost my independence.
But my! How pleased the people are!
(Including my descendants.)

Later

A new friend from way out West sent me this story.

A policeman found himself driving behind a car with four white-haired "li'l ol' ladies" going awfully slowly. He flashed his lights, and the car pulled over. When he walked up to it, the driver asked, "Was I doing anything wrong, officer?"

"No," he replied. "But driving too slow is as dangerous as driving too fast, and you were going *very* slowly."

"But the sign *says* 22," she answered.

"Oh, ma'am, that's the route sign, not the speed limit."

By this time he'd noticed the other three ladies were sitting very stiff and still, each one staring straight ahead. "Ladies, are you all right?" he asked. No answer; no one even moved.

He asked again, and finally the lady in the passenger seat said, "We just came off of Route 119."

12

Going Home

November 23rd

This morning I found Louly sitting in a chair, brushing her hair, and looking better.

"Hi, Hattie!" she said, sounding almost like her old self. "I'm glad to see you. I want to get out of this jail."

"Oh, Louly! Don't call it that! They're taking good care of you."

"I know it. I'm just kidding. But I *would* like to get dressed and go to the dining room for lunch. Could you engineer that?"

I said I thought I could. Sure enough, the head nurse gave permission for me to push my dear friend in a wheelchair to the familiar place where she had eaten so many hundreds of meals.

People greeted her warmly and at first she seemed to enjoy the attention; but after she had eaten only a few bites of her lunch, she put her fork down and refused to eat any more. She began to droop, noticeably. I think she must have had another slight stroke, because her eyes did not seem to focus right.

"Take me home. Please take me home," she said.

"Of course, Louly," I replied. "We'll go back to the Health Center right away."

"No. No! I mean, take me *home*...I need to go home...." Her eyes were looking really odd by now. She grabbed my hand. "I need to see Mama—and Theresa—and Papa—and Grandma." She clutched my hand, pleadingly. "I want to go *home*. Please help me!"

When we got her to bed, and quieted, the nurse agreed that she had probably had another stroke.

"Did I bring it on? Taking her to the dining room?" I asked afterwards, in the hall.

"No, indeed, Mrs. McNair. Don't blame yourself. The doctor has been expecting another incident. There will probably be more."

Oh, my. Poor, dear Louly. I will never forget the frightened look, the pleading in her voice as she begged to be taken back to the safe nest of her childhood. How I wish

I pushed my dear friend in a wheelchair to the familiar place where she had eaten so many hundreds of meals.

I could transport her there. All I can do is give her a hand to hold on to. I will try to do that more often.

The wish to "go home" seems to be a universal one in the Infirmary (as I'm afraid I will always call it). I've heard about one lady who gets up in the middle of many nights and takes her few things out of the chest of drawers and packs them in her suitcase. She says she must be ready when her son comes the next day to take her home. Oh, my. "The pity of it!"

December 1st

We had a long family weekend over Thanksgiving. My daughter Nancy got the whole crowd together (at her house in the daytime, at the motel at night), and it was most enjoyable. I hope I didn't reminisce too much, but my listeners seemed to enjoy hearing about their ancestors.

Sunday morning we were having a delicious pancake breakfast, and two of the young ones were pouring on more and more syrup. Trying to distract them, I announced that my father—their great-grandfather— would *never* put a drop of syrup on his pancakes.

"Why?" puzzled one of the children.

"I asked him that very question when I was about your age," I replied.

"'Child,' he told me, 'I had enough syrup at the Citadel to last me the rest of my life. Some days—in fact, a good many days—we had nothing to eat but biscuits and syrup all day.'"

My father had entered the Citadel (Charleston's famous military school) in 1883, the first year of its reopening after the Civil War. It had opened on a "shoestring," with barely enough money to pay the teachers a very small stipend. Toward the end of the month, grocery money would give out. There'd be meal after meal of biscuits and syrup.

"Did he graduate?" one of the grandchildren asked.

"'Deed he did!" I bragged. "And he became one of the most acclaimed hydroelectric engineers in the South. He built dams when dam-builders were feeling their way. It was a brand new industry."

I could tell that my children and "grands" were interested in this man they had never known. They had admired his portrait.

"Would you like to hear me brag some more about him?"

"Please do, Nana!"

"Well, let's see. My father was born in 1866 in Mt. Pleasant, South Carolina. His father had been a professor at the Citadel 'befo' th' waw' (as they say), served as a major in the Confederate Army, and died three years after the conflict ended. Those were hard, hard times in the South. There was a local one-room school that went through the eighth grade, and most of the young people in the small town were resigned to the fact that their education would end there. But not my father. He had a good mind, and was determined to better himself. Here's what he did:

"The woods just north of Mt. Pleasant were alive with birds, covey after covey of quail. Papa would get up at five o'clock every weekday morning and take his gun and his bird dog to the woods and shoot a goodly number of quail. (There was no limit in those days.)

"Then he would go home, get in his rowboat, and row across the harbor to Charleston, three miles. (There was no bridge then. There was a ferry, but he didn't have the fare.) He would take his birds to the Charleston Hotel and sell them to the chef for the guests' breakfasts. That way he made enough money for clothes and books and tuition at the Charleston High School. He graduated with honors and won a scholarship to the newly revived Citadel."

"He rowed across that harbor *every day?*" asked a grandchild.

"Five days a week," I said. "Over and back. When I heard the story as a little girl (not from him), I said, 'Papa, I don't see how you did it.'

"'Well, my hands would get right cold on winter mornings—but it wasn't too bad.'"

I looked around at my "flock" and wondered if any of my sire's ambitious genes and determination had been passed down.

"Tell us some more," said Bobby.

"Well, let's see...oh, I remember hearing Papa tell about taking a bath when he was a cadet. Each room in the barracks had a corner fireplace, a grate in which a coal fire was kept burning on winter days. There was no central heating, of course. On Saturday nights, if Papa had a date with a Charleston girl (it was called 'an engagement' in those days), he would put a cannonball on top of the coals. Then he'd bring buckets of water from a spigot down the hall and fill up his tin tub. Then, using the coal shovel, he would lift out the red-hot cannonball and put it in the tub. When the water was good and hot, he'd take the cannonball out, and get in.

"I hope that Charleston girl appreciated her clean cadet!" I added fervently.

Just before I left Nancy's at Thanksgiving, one of the female grandchildren said, "Nana, did Grandfather marry that Charleston girl?"

"No, honey, he didn't. He married my mother. I mean she *became* my mother. She was a girl from a tiny town called Clayton, Alabama."

"How did *that* happen? I mean, way back in their century I thought they always married a hometown girl, even if she was a cousin—with nobody having the money to travel—"

I had to laugh. "She wasn't a cousin, thank goodness. It was right interesting the way it came about. When Papa graduated from the Citadel he got a job as a surveyor with the Central of Georgia Railroad. They were expanding into Alabama. He first saw my mama upside down! She was picking flowers in her parents' yard on the edge of town, and he spied her through his surveying instrument. Was it called a transit? Anyway, he liked what he saw, even upside down. He managed to meet her, and six months later they were married. Wasn't that romantic?"

My seventeen-year-old granddaughter nodded and sighed. "Nothing romantic like that ever happens today."

December 2nd

I remember my grandmother using a cane, wearing a shawl in cool weather, and feeling for things that she couldn't see. I remember her walking up and down in front of the fireplace, her fingers probing every inch of the mantelpiece, looking for her eyeglasses.

I felt sorry for her; but I remember thinking: I will never get that way. I will go to doctors *early;* I will do things to ward off shaky legs and poor eyesight. *Never* will I let myself get in such a fix.

Hah! I now use a cane, wear a shawl on cold days, and grope for things that I can't see. I have noticed my granddaughter looking at me with definite pity in her eyes and with a little trace of something else. She will make sure that such deterioration doesn't happen to *her*.

Ah, the arrogance of youth.

~

A dear memory:

My hair turned gray early.

One day when I was about sixty, my eight-year-old granddaughter asked me to go bicycle riding with her.

"Oh, darling," I said, "I can't do that. I'm too old."

She looked at me hard. "You're not old, Nana. Your hair got old, but *you* didn't."

Bless her heart.

13

Quips and Trips

December 3rd

There has been a vacancy at our table since Lucius Grover died two weeks ago. Today someone we thought was a new resident came and sat down.

"I hope I'm not protruding," she said.

I was about to whoop with laughter, when I stopped short. Maybe she didn't know she meant "intrude." Maybe she wasn't being funny.... If only she had smiled when she said it.

She turned out to be a visitor, not a new resident, and perhaps she had confused "pro" with "in," but she made her statement in a lovely, well-modulated voice that charmed me.

Voices are important to me—maybe too much so. There are people who are interesting and knowledge-able—yet I want nothing to do with them because of the tone of their voices.

I'm extremely allergic to certain women's voices—women who are completely grown up but who still talk like little girls. No matter what they are saying, I seem to hear, "Ooh-ee! Ooh-ee! Listen to itsy-bitsy me. Aren't I cute?"

That's terrible of me. Some of them are perfectly nice, mature people. I am too critical. I just wish that they had been exposed to some kind of voice therapy, or that a little *mezzo* had been trained into their *soprano* rendi-tions. Sometimes when one friend of mine is talking, the words seem to go higher and higher—*coloratura*—as if they are going to fly out of the top of her head. I wonder if she has ever heard herself on audio tape?... Maybe I could arrange something.... (No, Dear Diary, I won't, I promise.)

December 5th

Overheard:

Geneva, going down the hall this morning, muttering:

"Bad eyes, bad ears, bad knees, bad back...but I'll tell you one thing: there's nothing wrong with my tongue. I can still talk, and I'm *goin'* to."

Geneva's right about her tongue, and everyone else's. You never hear of a tongue virus, or a sprained tongue or a dislocated tongue. And considering the mileage, that's a wonder.

A truism: As the deterioration of old age sets in, the first thing to go is the screw that controls the tongue. Oh, me.

Later

Another amusing "take" on aging appeared in our *Family Affairs* newsletter. I guess, Dear Diary, these observations shouldn't seem amusing to those of us to whom they apply. But I can't help it. Laughing at tribulations seems much healthier than crying!

Here are a few ways to know your "Golden Years" have arrived:

When you stop wearing your girdle and high-heeled shoes because you realize no one is looking anymore.

When waitresses give you the senior discount and you don't even ask.

When you have your seventh grandchild and stop coloring your hair.

When you see a highway sign that reads, "Forgive and forget. It will add years to your life," and you turn to your spouse and tell him you are getting so good at the forgetting part you may live forever.

When everything you have has started either leaking or drying up.

When you kiss your husband and he yawns.

When you realize quality is more important than quantity.

When you realize your children belong to the AARP.

When your little black book contains mostly names ending in M.D.

When everything hurts and what doesn't, doesn't work.

When you get winded playing chess.

When your children begin to look middle-aged.

When you join a health club, but can't go.

When you know all the answers, but no one asks the questions.

When you look forward to a dull evening.

When you sit in a rocking chair and can't get started.

When your knees buckle and your belt won't.

When dialing long distance wears you out.

When your back goes out more than you do.
When you sink your teeth into a steak and
they stay there.

December 6th

Paul and Curtis were sitting on the terrace this unseasonably mild afternoon, smoking and talking after Sunday dinner. And I was perched near the library window, eavesdropping as usual.

"I've got a joke to tell you, Paul," said Curtis. "An old pal at home calls me every so often, and he has a great sense of humor. See if you like this:

"Three friends were in a car crash. They were killed, and went to heaven. The next day an angel said to their spirits, 'Down below, you are now in your caskets, and people are looking at you. What do you hope they are saying?'

"The first man said, 'I hope they are saying that I was a fine citizen.'

"The second man said, 'I hope they're saying I was a good husband and father.'

"The third man was quiet. The angel prompted him, 'What about you?'

"The man grinned and said, 'I hope they're saying, "Look!! He's still moving!"'"

December 7th

Today I was walking behind two men in Main Hall, and heard one say to the other:

"I guess I'm like that fellow that sang the song in *Show Boat:* 'I'm tired of livin', an' feared of dyin'.'"

Well, I thought, at least he's honest.

After the two gentlemen-residents left the lunch table today, we remaining females began to talk about our husbands—all of whom had to be modified by a sad adjective: our *late* husbands.

All of a sudden it hit me that we were being rude, because one of our number, Trina Montgomery, had never been married. She saw me looking at her worriedly, and she grinned.

"Don't mind about me," she said. "You see, my husband died in infancy."

Good old Trina.

One person told this story about a woman in another retirement home who, after her husband died, went to the local undertaker to make arrangements for her own funeral.

"My husband is buried in Arlington Cemetery," she told the man, "and I want to be buried beside him. You will have to make arrangements with the railway company about shipping my body."

"Oh, don't worry," said the undertaker. "We'll send you by plane."

"No, you won't," said the lady emphatically. "I don't fly."

~

Later, I recalled a memorable trip I once made by airplane.

When the last child finished college, Sam and I decided to celebrate with a long-awaited trip to Europe. What great memories I have of that month! One unforgettable event is funny now, but it was quite mortifying at the time.

Friends had clued me in that toilet tissue was not always furnished in parts of Europe; and that when it *was* furnished, instead of being "soft as old linen," it often felt about as soft as old scrap iron. So, to be safe, I put a small roll of pale pink Charmin in my large handbag.

When we reached our *pension* in Paris, Sam told me to put on my best finery, for we were going to the Ritz Hotel for tea. Sam had spent one night at the Ritz, long ago, and he wanted me to have a taste of its elegance.

We dressed up, took a taxi, and entered the famed hostelry. We stood in the lobby a moment, gazing at the Old World opulence and getting our bearings. I reached into my bag for a handkerchief, and guess what fell out?

Not only fell out but rolled across the lobby, leaving a pink trail? The Charmin.

I wished later that I had dashed out of the door before the heads started turning toward me. Instead, Sam and I stood, shocked and rooted to the spot. The next thing I knew a beautifully uniformed bellman had dashed to the end of the pink trail, rolled up the tissue neatly while dozens of people watched, and handed it to me with a bow. "Madame," he said, very formally.

Madame blushed scarlet and made the quickest exit of her life.

Now, when people talk about "the food at The Ritz" I can't add to the conversation. But I could tell them something about the service at The Ritz. It's *too* good.

I reached into my bag for a handkerchief,
and guess what fell out, leaving a pink trail?

14

Quizzes and Quotes

December 8th

The mail today brought three "fan letters," including two delightful amusements, from readers in completely different parts of the country. The quizzes gave me an afternoon of pleasant mental exercise (even though I came up with failing grades on both).

The first was a "Bible Quiz" which I tackled *confidently.* I tried to work it by circling groups of letters (not always in the same word) that spell out books of the Bible. But I only found the names of six of the sixteen books of scripture that are hidden in the text. I went to my Bible and studied the list of books, but I have to report that ten of the concealed titles eluded me. I'm mortified.

The second puzzler involved automobile names, so I don't feel quite so sheepish about not knowing all of them. I do know just who I want to show this quiz to first: Paul, our car-naming champion.

Here are the two quizzes. I will tuck the answers away in the back of the book.

QUIZ #1—BIBLE QUIZ

In the following passage, can you find the names of sixteen books of the Bible?

I once made a remark about the hidden books of the BIBLE. It was a lulu, kept people looking so hard for facts and for others it was a revelation. Some were in a jam, especially since the names of the books were not capitalized, but the truth finally struck home to numbers of readers. To others, it was a real job. We want it to be a most fascinating few moments for you. YES, THERE WILL BE SOME REALLY EASY ONES TO SPOT. Others may require judges to help them. I will quickly admit it usually takes a minister to find one of them, and there will be loud lamentations when it is found. A little lady says she brews a cup of tea so she can concentrate better. See how well you can compete. Relax now, for there are really sixteen books of the Bible in this story.

QUIZ #2—WHICH CARS DO YOU REMEMBER?

1. A famous Indian chief _____
2. A kind of rock used for striking fire _____
3. The crossing of a stream _____
4. An intoxicated maker of bread _____
5. A city in Texas _____
6. A French general _____
7. A gentle breeze _____
8. A Spanish explorer _____
9. A French explorer _____
10. Ancient + a letter + city in Alabama _____
11. Male deer plus one letter _____
12. A rock famous in American history _____
13. To grind the teeth in anger _____
14. A river in New York _____
15. Honest U.S. president _____
16. A river in the Holy Land _____
17. Across country _____
18. A satellite _____

19. A kind of cracker _____
20. Rip an aircraft _____
21. A high ecclesiastic _____
22. A heavenly body _____
23. Michigan city _____
24. A French racing driver _____
25. A planet _____
26. A jungle cat _____
27. A brand of coffee _____
28. If really tired, you're all _____ ed out.
29. Former title of German ruler _____
30. Kite-flying diplomat _____

December 8th

A dear old friend sent me a lovely Christmas card. Her message:

> I say, with the poet, may it be that
> "...thou hast no sorrow in thy song,
> No winter in thy year."

What poet is she quoting, I wonder? Since I don't like sad songs *or* cold weather, I appreciate the sentiment.

Later this evening after the news I was going through a box of papers and found some of my own poetical efforts from days gone by:

DEFINITION

Sang-froid: the power to maintain
A look of calm repose
When a splinter on the church's seat
Has torn your nylon hose.

And this bit of terse verse:

MARRIAGE VOWS
(To Have, to Hold, and to Zip)

June brides are getting promises.
For one more they should press:
That he should promise always to
Zip up the back of her dress!

Zipping is still a problem, even with the gadgets people have invented to try to help. But old age has brought new worries when it comes to getting dressed—worries that those "June brides" don't have. I've complained to you before, Dear Diary: Maybe the reason I have so many hang-ups about the way I look is because there are so many hang-*downs*. Oh, me.

December 9th

I have an appointment with my eye doctor after the holidays. As my world dims, I want the lights to be stronger everywhere. I want 200-watt bulbs in all lamps. I want sunshine streaming in. More light might help. More light!

I take to myself, in comfort, a verse in Revelation:

> And there shall be no night there; and they need no candle, neither light of the sun; for the Lord God giveth the light....

...And I will see again!

December 15th

Last Saturday Arthur and Artie and Cliffie, along with Mr. C, brought in a large, fresh Christmas tree and set it up at one end of our dining room. Today we were told that the Program Department is doing something different this year. Instead of the staff decorating it, as usual, they want us to "dress it" ourselves.

Lurline, our program director, said, "We will finish up the decorating with tinsel and 'snow'; but we want you-all, first, to place on the tree any decoration that you want to. We would prefer that it be an ornament that has meaning, that has a story behind it; and we want you to tell us the story, on Friday night."

We looked at one another a little uncertainly; but Lurline and her assistant, Sophie, are so good to us—so patient with our orneryness and strange requests—that we felt we had to go along with them.

"Don't forget, now," Lurline said as we broke up, "bring something you love—something with meaning—and with a story."

December 16th

We had a cold and wet blast from Old Man Winter today. It was the kind of day when you try to avoid going outside at all.

When I walk these days—whether inside or outside—I plant each foot: plunk, plunk, *so* carefully. I will *not* be a Fallen Woman.

∼

Overheard:

Two ladies were walking down the hall. One of them said, "Honey, these days—or nights—I'm scared to go to sleep for fear I'll wake up dead!"

December 17th

I have been trying to clear out some of the clutter in my apartment, so that when I have to move to the Assisted Living Department or to the Health Care Center (where most residents here end their days) there will not be such a "hooraw's nest" for my children to tackle.

It's not an easy task. I've scaled down before, but this is, perhaps, the last "ridding" I will do, and it hurts—especially when it comes to my books.

How can I part with my own inscribed seventy-five-year-old copy of *A Child's Garden of Verses?* Or the books that Mother read to me: *Uncle Remus, The Little Colonel, Little Lord Fauntleroy, Miss Minerva and William Green Hill,* and *Diddie, Dumps and Tot?* To say nothing of books that I collected as an adult: *Meditations* by Marcus Aurelius, *The Screwtape Letters,* and my collection of *The World's Most Famous Letters?*

I will keep my Bible (in large print), my dictionary, my thesaurus, and three books of poetry, even if I can't read any of them anymore without a strong magnifying lamp. And I will try not to grieve.

In going through the books this morning I found a battered little brown volume that had belonged to my parents, called *Songs, Merry and Sad.* It is by a young North Carolina poet who wrote in the early years of this century: John Charles McNeill. What an hour of reveling I had! I laughed and cried, and felt sorry that this rare talent inhabited our Southern world for such a short time. (He died quite young.) What an ear and eye he had! What a heart, and voice! I wish I could quote pages and pages here. A small sample:

LOVE'S FASHION

Oh, I can jest with Margaret
  And laugh a gay good-night,
But when I take my Helen's hand
  I dare not clasp it tight.

I dare not hold her dear white hand
  More than a quivering space,
And I should bless a breeze that blew
  Her hair into my face.

'Tis Margaret I call sweet names:
  Helen is too, too dear
For me to stammer little words
  Of love into her ear.

So now, good night, fair Margaret,
  And kiss me ere we part!
But one dumb touch of Helen's hand,
  And oh, my heart, my heart!

(Move over, A. E. Housman!)

And another one, where he is writing from the point of view of a sharecropper. (I can see the tired horse and driver, going home in the gathering dusk.)

HARVEST

Cows in the stall and sheep in the fold;
Clouds in the west, deep crimson and gold;
A heron's far flight to a roost somewhere;
The twitter of killdeer keen in the air;
The noise of a wagon that jolts through the gloam
On the last load home.

There are lights in the windows; a blue spire of smoke
Climbs from the grange grove of elm and oak.
The smell of the Earth, where the light pours to her
Its dewy libation, is sweeter than myrrh,
And an incense to Toil is the smell of the loam
On the last load home.

I could not find a poem of his that I remembered
from long ago. It must have been in his other book of
poetry. (He published two.)
I recall two lines:

I gits my chillun up 'fore day
'Cause de dew, it makes de cotton weigh.

I could see the little shirt-tailed figures being hurried
into the field in the dark, because the wet cotton they
would pick would lie heavier on the scales. What pic-
tures and feelings that young man could conjure up!

I hope the spirit of John Charles McNeill met up in heaven with the shades of two Roberts: Burns and Stevenson. I like to think of the three of them, lolling on the banks of some ethereal Sweet Afton, flowing gently while they swap lighthearted celestial observations.

I am adding the name of John Charles McNeill to the list of gifted, funny, greathearted, lyrical souls I hope to encounter in the "sweet by-and-by."

Perhaps I should hang a book on the tree! But, no, I actually found something that I had all but forgotten. I'll take it to the tree-trimming, and perhaps I'll pass it along after the holidays to one of my children and include the story behind it.

15

Around the Tree

December 18th

We came together in the dining room tonight to "trim" the Christmas tree. (I wonder why they call it "trimming"?)

Our two program directors welcomed us, and said that, with Arthur's help, they had found the large, symmetrical, live tree. We were glad about *not* using one of The Home's artificial trees.

The fragrance took me back to those wonderful December days when I would go with my father to cut our tree, on a cousin's farm.

There was a nice crowd for the evening, including Louly. An aide brought her in a wheelchair and rolled her up beside me. I'm not too sure how much of the festivities she took in. She is a mere shadow of herself, but does not seem to be in any pain. I believe my dear friend is just worn out and is ready to go whenever she is called.

We opened by singing "Oh Come, All Ye Faithful, Joyful and Triumphant." Then Lurline asked us to bring up our ornaments, one at a time.

We were hesitant. Nobody wanted to be first, it seemed. Then, to our surprise, Henry Holston got up.

Henry came here about three years ago with his wife, who soon "turned funny" (as they used to say about old people) and had to be put in the Health Care Center. Not long after that, Henry, who seemed lost, began to "turn funny," too. He still lives in their apartment, but his days there are numbered because he gets disoriented. He doesn't always know what month it is, much less what day.

But here he was, going up to the front. He carried two objects tied together with a string, and wrapped around and around with tinsel. He held the objects up.

"The ladies said to bring something we loved, to put on the tree. Well, these are my bedroom slippers. I love 'em. They feel good. They fit my toes just right. I want to hang 'em on the tree." And he did, placing the string across a limb.

I saw Lurline and Sophie look at each other in dismay. This wasn't exactly what they had envisioned. However, they rose to the occasion nobly.

"Thank you, Mr. Holston," said Sophie, not cracking a smile.

"You're welcome," he said, seeming pleased.

One of the men sang out, "What are you going to do for slippers, Henry?"

"I'll manage," he said, sitting down, and smiling. (Oh, the intricacies of the deteriorating mind! We are met with examples of them here that could fill a new textbook.)

I was struck with the fact that there was no tittering as the old gentleman sat down. There is so much kindness here. I see it on all sides, among the residents as well as the staff. We speak of TLC, Tender Loving Care. I also like to speak of P&K: Patience and Kindness.

Sophie turned to me, a tiny trace of desperation in her voice. "Miss Hattie, do you have something?"

I made my way to the front, holding my tissue-wrapped ornament.

"I can't believe I've kept this for nearly seventy years! It's a little beat-up now, but it still has meaning for me.

"For three summers when I was a youngster—eleven, twelve, and thirteen—my parents sent me to a girls' summer camp high up in North Carolina's topography: a place called Little Switzerland, nestled in the tip-top of the Blue Ridge Mountains.

"My little tent-mate was miserable. A 'sand-lapper' from lower South Carolina, she said the mountains scared her. I loved them. To me they weren't brood-ing—just majestic and mysterious.

"The village of Little Switzerland consisted of a coun-try store, a tiny post office, an inn, and a church. It was two miles from the camp, and we were allowed to walk to the store on Saturday afternoons.

"Amid the conglomeration in the store—washtubs, bolts of cloth, harnesses, barrels of apples, lanterns, etc.—there was only one thing that interested us: the candy counter. There was no choice at the candy counter; just Hershey bars. Fortunately, we liked Hershey bars enough to walk two miles, both ways, to get them.

"But one Saturday afternoon the candy counter was empty. Our hearts sank. We approached the storekeeper timidly. (He was a dour soul.)

"'Did you know you were out of Hershey bars?' I asked.

"'Yep.'

"'Aren't you going to get some more?'

"'Nope.'

"'Why *not?*'

"'Sell out too fast,' he said.

"It happened. I'll swear to it.

"But that day, while wandering around the store dejectedly, I spied something unusual on a counter: this little wreath."

I unwrapped the tissue and held it up.

"As you can see, it is made of small leather hearts, stuffed and strung together. Between each two hearts is a cluster of beads. The beads are berries (I think), painted over heavily in bright red. It intrigued me, and I asked the proprietor who made it.

"'There's a family of Indians that live a few miles from here. One of their girls made that, and asked me to sell it for her. It's two dollars.'

"I had that much in my allowance, and now I didn't even have candy bars to spend it on, so I bought the wreath. It has been on every tree I've had, every Christmas since then. I handle it with care, and think of the Indian girl who cut and stuffed the leather hearts and painted the beads. I do hope she had some fun with her two dollars."

I hung the little wreath lovingly on the tree.

Cora Hunter went to the front next, holding up a shining object by a silver chain. It consisted of three small crystal angels. Each angel held to the chain with one hand while her other hand clutched a tiny harp. Cora held it high. It was lovely.

"If I tell you the story of this ornament you will know how old I am.... Oh, well, what the heck! It was 1919, and I was six years old.

"A lady on our street, a widow named Mrs. Preston, bought a car and learned to drive it: two unusual things for a woman to do in our little town at that time.

"Someone would yell, 'She's comin' by!' and we would dash to the front yard to watch the car creep by, with Mrs. Preston stiff-armed at the steering wheel. I don't think she ever went more than eight miles an hour.

"She called it 'the limousine,' and I guess it was, but it looked more like a glassed-in box—straight up and down. She could have bought a 'touring car,' but instead she bought the fanciest job Ford made at that time. It even had vases on the walls for flowers (which she kept filled), and tiny window shades with fringe.

"Since Mrs. Preston lived just two doors from us, and since she seemed lonely, I would go to see her sometimes. I kept hoping she would take me for a ride in her grand car, but I think she was afraid of the responsibility.

"One Christmas she gave me this lovely thing." Cora held it up to the light. It tinkled as she shook it. "Mrs. Preston said she had bought it to hang in a window of 'the limousine,' but decided that the roughness of her starting and stopping might break it; so she wanted me to hang it on our tree and enjoy it and keep it.

"Oh, how I *have* enjoyed it, every single year. Some of you here have seen it on the tiny artificial tree in my room. I will try to find a safe place for it here—and, please, please, don't anybody shake the tree!"

She hung her little angels in a secluded spot on the tree, and we gave Cora and her treasured ornament a big hand.

Graham McKnight walked up close to the tree and held up a bag from which he took a small, well-worn book.

"This is the first book I ever found under a Christmas tree with my name on it. There were many more in later years, but I can remember the thrill of getting this first one, inscribed to me. It's *The Wizard of Oz*, and I was eight years old that Christmas.

"About a year later my mother took me to the library and got me a card. That opened the road to *Treasure Island*, the Rover Boys, Tom Sawyer, and all the other magical people and places; but this was the very first book of my very own. I've treasured it through the years—partly because of my mother's handwritten message in the front—and I'll be happy to see it on our tree."

We clapped as he placed the beloved little volume between two limbs.

Rose and Louise took us all back to our childhoods with the chains they had made. They had colored sheets of notepaper with red and green crayons, cut the paper into strips, and pasted the strips around each other, into long chains. They placed the chains lovingly on the tree.

Then Sidney and Retta offered their contribution: a basket full of something fluffy and white—a popcorn chain!

"We popped corn in our microwave," said Sidney, "and spent last evening stringing the kernels together."

"It was fun," said Retta. "Took me back about ninety-five years!"

They draped their handiwork proudly around the tree.

Somebody (I can't remember who) added a wreath they had made out of pyracantha berries. Somebody else added several cups, handmade from gold paper, and filled with candy.

Then came Bill Nixon with one of the best ideas of all. He said, "I remembered that we always had 'live' candles on our tree. My father lit them every Christmas morning and I can remember how big-eyed we were at the sight. He always kept buckets of water close by.

"I had trouble locating these candleholders, but I finally found some at an antiques store in Charleston, and found these candles at Wal-Mart. As you can see, I brought two buckets of water, just in case."

Lurline and Sophie helped him clamp the candleholders to limbs around the tree, and helped to light the candles. When we turned off the overhead lights, a chorus of "Ooo-ooo! How lovely!" went up. I saw some tears on some cheeks, especially after we sang "Silent Night," very softly.

We sang one verse of "It Came Upon the Midnight Clear." Nobody could remember the other verses; but after we broke up and went to our rooms, I looked up that carol in my hymn book. I knew there were some lines in it that applied to people under stress, including the very real stress that my aged, aching friends and I were trying to bear up under.

I found the verse:

> And ye, beneath life's crushing load,
> Whose forms are bending low,
> Who toil along the climbing way
> With painful steps and slow,
> Look now! For glad and golden hours
> Come swiftly on the wing;
> O rest beside the weary road
> And hear the angels sing.

December 20th

There is a song heard this season that really gets under my skin. I was inspired to write the following:

TOO OFT-OCCURRING CAROL

> I love the Yule season
>   Until—"heah he cum":
> That drum-beating boy with his
>   Rump-a-pum-pum.
>
> The song's gentle message
>   Is quite overcome
> By that ever monotonous
>   Rump-a-pum-pum.

> I wish that nice boy
>> With his tuneless pum-pum
> Had studied the lyre
>> Instead of the drum.

December 27th

Another lovely Christmas, Dear Diary, with a house full of my descendants. I am blessed.

December 30th

Several of us are trying to plan a "do" of some kind for New Year's Eve tomorrow night. But I don't believe many of the residents can stay awake till midnight. We may have to change the hands on the big wall clock a little!

*When we turned off the overhead lights, a chorus of
"Ooo-ooo! How lovely!" went up.*

16

No Coward Soul

January 5th

My eye doctor shook his head. He had examined the fronts and backs of both my eyes with every pertinent instrument.

"It's worse, isn't it?" I asked. "The macula has degenerated some more, hasn't it?"

He nodded sadly.

"Is anybody *doing* anything about it?" I wailed. "Since more and more people seem to have the sickening thing?"

"Oh, yes! Night and day," he assured me. "The thing they're working on hardest is a plan to use fetal tissue—the umbilical cord, in fact—that they think will revitalize the retina."

That may not be exactly what he said, but anyway I got the gist of it, and it fostered a tiny bit of hope in the heart of this Poor Old Soul, whose world is getting dimmer by the day.

I have just two words to say to those dedicated scientists working on the project: *Please hurry.*

January 7th

I have been deeply touched lately by the kindness of "all hands" toward me, since my eyesight has failed.

It is truly heartwarming. They seem to outdo each other in watching out for the Poor Old Soul—and not just the paid staff. The residents, too, seem determined that Hattie shall not fall down, or go in the wrong door, or open the wrong mailbox. They are *so* ready and willing to read the menu to me, to help me sign a check, to look up words in the dictionary, and even to help me answer letters. I don't have to ask. Folks offer. They think up ways to help me.

Their genuine and helpful kindness, beyond the call of duty, has had a softening effect on my aged heart. *Truly!* I am overwhelmed by the goodness of people.

All people? Well, I like to think that I live in "God's Country," which is un*doubt*edly the Southern part of the United States of America; and there is a marked gentility in these parts. But we have some people here at The Home who, through no fault of their own, were born above the Mason-Dixon Line, and I have to admit that they are just as kind to me as the "bawn" Southerners.

Robert Burns wrote about "man's inhumanity to man." Well, I suppose there's plenty of that; but lately I have witnessed just the opposite. So much humanity has been demonstrated to me that the thought of it makes my throat ache.

Tennyson said, "Kind hearts are more than coronets." Oh, they are, they are. I'm finding that out every day, now that I have to be on the receiving end of kindness.

I love "those dear hearts and gentle people...."

I'm reminded of a song that we sang in Sunday School long ago:

> Little deeds of kindness
> Little words of love
> Make the earth an Eden
> Like the heaven above.

I didn't really know what I was singing about, then. I do now.

January 8th

My prayer list is getting longer all the time, alas. As soon as somebody gets better and I can take them off, there's somebody else to put on.

In my feeble state, there may come a time when I'll

have to stop listing all the people and causes, and just say: "Lord, you know who they all are. You've heard me name them so many times. Bless them all, I humbly pray."

And sometimes I think, "Who am I to be asking *Him* to do *any*thing?"

Speaking of prayers, someone sent me a funny one yesterday:

A PRAYER

(written by that prolific guy, Anonymous)
Dear God,
So far today, I've done all right.
I haven't gossiped.
I haven't lost my temper.
I haven't been greedy.
I haven't been grumpy.
I haven't been nasty.
I haven't been selfish.
I haven't been overindulgent.
For this I am very thankful.

However, in a few minutes, God,
I am going to get out of bed, and from then on,
I'm probably going to need a lot more help.
Amen.

One of the nicest prayers, I think, was written by that softhearted man, Robert Louis Stevenson, who gave us such a wealth of beautifully expressed feeling in his books—from his *A Child's Garden of Verses* to his *Requiem.*

THE CELESTIAL SURGEON

If I have faltered more or less
In my great task of happiness;
If I have moved among my race
And shown no glorious morning face;
If beams from happy human eyes
Have moved me not; if morning skies,
Books, and my food, and summer rain
Knocked on my sullen heart in vain;
Lord, thy most pointed pleasure take
And stab my spirit broad awake.

January 10th

There was a wonderful old movie on television this cold, wintry afternoon: Emily Brontë's *Wuthering Heights.* It was a delight watching Sir Laurence Olivier, such a *young* (and handsome) Sir Laurence. And the beautiful Merle Oberon.

Those "Brontë girls," especially Charlotte and Emily, have always been an intriguing mystery to me. Raised in a dreary manse, in a remote hamlet, with a stern widowed father and an alcoholic brother, they somehow managed to keep a lamp burning. With little formal education, no

writing lessons—not even English Composition 101—
they managed to bring forth structured novels that have
stood the test of time: *Jane Eyre* as well as *Wuthering
Heights*. They even had to sign men's names to their man-
uscripts to get them looked at by a publisher.

Sometimes, "while life's dark maze I tread," when "the
days grow short as you reach September," and when, in
spite of much good stuff, there are doubts and fears, I
think of the first lines of a prayer that Emily Brontë
wrote so bravely, from her bleak habitat:

> No coward soul is mine,
> No trembler in the world's storm-troubled sphere:
> I see Heaven's glories shine,
> And faith shines equal, arming me from fear.

What a woman!

January 13th

In my last entry I quoted some words from an old
hymn ("My Faith Looks Up to Thee"):

> While life's dark maze I tread
> And griefs around me spread....

In a retirement community there are griefs a-plenty:
seeing decline, seeing friends go down in sometimes
pitiful ways.

Once in a great while you see somebody go up! Truly! They've been living alone, not eating properly, maybe being worried by householders' frustrations—and they come here and start to gain weight and to "pick up"! Maybe they've been lonely, too, like Mr. Cruickshank. Anyway, it's good to see them mingling and eating— and *laughing*. It makes you know these "homes" are worthwhile places.

January 18th

Taste. Good taste. Is it inborn, or cultivated? Maybe what is inborn would get some cultivation if we followed the poet Goethe's advice: "One ought, every day at least, to hear a little song, read a good poem, see a fine picture, and, if possible, to speak a few reasonable words."

It wasn't the kind of "picture" that Goethe meant, but I did see a "fine" *moving* picture last night. (I am especially thankful for Public Television in winter. I often settle in front of an excellent program or movie, staying warm and dry inside, accompanied by a lovely pot of tea and a sandwich or plate of cookies.)

I watched another oldie called *The Yearling*, and when it was through I was a basket case. I had used at least ten tissues to mop up the buckets of tears, and I was emotionally exhausted.

I believe there are codes, now, marking certain movies too explicit or raw for children to see. Maybe there should be a code warning rickety old people that the movie is sad, tragic, pitiful, capable of bringing on a debilitating flood of tears.

The story is about a little boy on a remote farm a long time ago whose only playmate was a little deer. When his parents made him shoot that yearling, I couldn't *stand* it.

The thing was so skillfully done, so believable, that no heart could be unmoved; but oh, dear, the wracking sadness of it has stayed with me hours later.

Maybe the tear-shedding was therapeutic. I don't know. I can't get the little boy's—Jody's— sweet face out of my mind.

Thank goodness for one bright spot. Jody had Gregory Peck for a father.

January 23rd

A friend sent me this story. Maybe it is as long-eared as the mule, but I had never heard it.

Two bachelor brothers in the Dutch Fork area of South Carolina bought a new mule. The mule was con- siderably taller than the last one they owned.

As they were putting the new mule in their barn for the first time, his ears hit the top of the stall door. They were concerned that the constant scraping as he went in and out might hurt the mule's ears.

They discussed the problem. One brother said they'd

have to cut out a section over the stall door. The other brother disagreed and said it would be easier to shovel out a trench that the mule could walk in, rather than cut out above the door.

The first brother quickly rejected that solution, explaining emphatically, "That won't work! It's his ears that're too long, not his legs!"

February 4th

Vespers are held every Sunday evening here at The Home. The service, held in our beautiful chapel, consists of hymns, a short homily by a resident, and a prayer. Many relish it as a fitting way to end the Sabbath.

Last Sunday night was an exception. You see, it was Superbowl Sunday. The Vespers Committee figured that most of the residents would be in front of the TVs in their rooms, watching the game, so they tried a new ploy to get them out. They announced in our weekly paper, *Family Affairs,* that everyone was invited to the dining room at six o'clock where they could watch the game together on the extra-large screen. During the commercials the sound would be turned off, and a short service would be held.

A nice crowd turned out. They sang a hymn during the preliminaries. Emily had prepared a short message about two traits that are valuable in a home for the elderly: sympathy and understanding. She rose to give it during the second commercial; but there was a hitch, caused by the fact that one of the sponsors of the Superbowl was Victoria's Secret: the people who make the filmy, feminine underthings that leave few secrets untold.

Emily stood in front of the large, silent screen, giving her prepared talk. Behind her head, female figures, largely unclothed, pranced and pirouetted. "Sympathy and Understanding" lost out to long legs, bare skin, and silky nothings. Emily saw where all the eyes were fixed— especially the male eyes—and she gave up the battle.

I have a feeling that Vespers will be skipped next year on Superbowl Sunday.

February 8th

Today was an icy, winter day, and I stayed in the warm comfort of my apartment. I was lazy all day, though in the morning I wrote a few notes and paid some bills at my beautiful little desk. It gives me such pleasure to know that one day Amanda, and perhaps a daughter of hers, will sit in that lovely "lady's chair," at that very desk, many years hence.

This afternoon I settled into my "reading rocker" with my magnifying light at full power to check over the paperwork I did this morning. With my poor eyesight, I must be so careful, especially writing checks.

Then I spent a pleasurable spell browsing through some loved poetry and through my own musings and jottings of the past year. A particular entry from last July caught my attention, Dear Diary, when I was in a "stew" over mismatched earrings. I feel I must make a change, or at least an amendment to my railings about old age's failings.

I had written the line "Old Age, thy name is Pitiful." And old age *is* sickening in many ways, embarrassing and frustrating. As Shakespeare said it, in *Macbeth:*

> ...My way of life
> Is fall'n into the sere, the yellow leaf;
> And that which should accompany old age,
> As honour, love, obedience, troops of friends,
> I must not look to have....

Maybe Shakespeare's expectations were too high. Like most people, all I really want is to be able to get along, not to stumble. We have always been in charge, and suddenly (or so it seems) we are unsteady about everything—and don't want to admit it. Don't want anybody to notice it.

But it's *time* for unsteadiness to start, in the Great Plan, and we might as well relax and enjoy it. En*joy* it? Well, maybe enjoy a few little things like Senior Citizens' discounts, and people opening doors for us, etc.

Anyway, maybe I went too far in calling Old Age piti-ful, just because of a fashion *faux pas*. When all is said and done, I'm having a pretty good time in my ninth decade, in spite of the leaf being sere and yellow. Maybe a new leaf will come, one more time.

The End

Answers to Quizzes

ANSWERS TO THE BIBLE QUIZ

I once made a re<u>mark</u> about the hidden books of the BIBLE. It was a lu<u>lu, kep</u>t people loo<u>king s</u>o hard for <u>facts</u> and for others it was a <u>revelation</u>. Some were in a <u>jam, e</u>specially since the names of the books were not capitalized, but the t<u>ruth</u> finally struck home to <u>numbers</u> of readers. To others, it was a real <u>job</u>. We want it to be <u>a most</u> fascinating few moments for you. Y<u>ES, THERE</u> WILL BE SOME REALLY EASY ONES TO SPOT. Others may require <u>judges</u> to help them. I will quickly admi<u>t it u</u>sually takes a minister to find one of them, and there will be loud <u>lamentations</u> when it is found. A little lady says s<u>he brews</u> a cup of tea so she can concentrate better. See how well you can comp<u>ete. R</u>elax now, for there are really sixteen books of the Bible in this story.

ANSWERS TO THE CAR QUIZ

1. Pontiac
2. Flint
3. Ford
4. Studebaker
5. Austin
6. Lafayette
7. Zephyr
8. DeSoto
9. LaSalle
10. Oldsmobile
11. Buick
12. Plymouth
13. Nash
14. Hudson
15. Lincoln
16. Jordan
17. Overland
18. Moon
19. Graham
20. Terraplane
21. Pope
22. Star
23. Cadillac
24. Chevrolet
25. Mercury
26. Jaguar
27. Maxwell
28. Tucker
29. Kaiser
30. Franklin

A NOTE FROM THE EDITORS

This book was selected by the Book and Inspirational Media Division of the company that publishes *Guideposts*, a monthly magazine filled with true stories of people's adventures in faith.

Guideposts is available by subscription. All you have to do is write to Guideposts, 39 Seminary Hill Road, Carmel, New York 10512. When you subscribe, each month you can count on receiving exciting new evidence of God's presence, His guidance and His limitless love for all of us.

Guideposts is also available on the Internet by accessing our home page on the World Wide Web at www.guideposts.org. Send prayer requests to our Monday morning Prayer Fellowship. Read stories from recent issues of our magazines, *Guideposts*, *Angels on Earth*, *Guideposts for Kids*, and *Guideposts for Teens*, and follow our popular book of devotionals, *Daily Guideposts*. Excerpts from some of our best-selling books are also available.